PRAISE

"Thor, Baldacci, Flynn, Hamburg. Get ready as Banner fits right in!"

AMAZON REVIEW

"Move over Jack Reacher there's a new guy taking over."

AMAZON REVIEW

"Great stuff. Exciting and fast paced. On par with Flynn & Thor."

AMAZON REVIEW

"The writing was superior, the story line was compelling and the action was top-notch. Sorry I could only give this one a five star rating!"

AMAZON REVIEW

BLOODY RETRIBUTION
A HARRY BAUER THRILLER

BLAKE BANNER

RIGHTHOUSE

ISBN-13: 978-1-63696-327-3

ISBN-10: 1-63696-327-7

Cover design by: Damonza

Printed in the United States of America

www.righthouse.com

www.instagram.com/righthousebooks

www.facebook.com/righthousebooks

twitter.com/righthousebooks

HARRY BAUER THRILLER SERIES

ONE

I WAS UP AT THE BAR AT CARLOW EAST, LOOKING DOWN at a pint of Guinness and a shot of Bushmills chaser. It was three in the morning. I was feeling sorry for myself, and the Irish guy who was wiping down the bar wasn't helping. Barmen should be like therapists. They should listen, not talk, and they should make empathetic faces and noises. This guy didn't get it.

"Sure, and didn't I get home and find her in our matrimonial bed with my own brother? And didn't she run home to her feckin' mother and blame me for neglecting her? While me own brother sits and quotes feckin' Milton at me. An English poet, for Christ's sake. 'Sean,' he says, 'It's all about perspective,' he says. 'The mind is its own place, and can make a heaven of hell, and a hell of heaven. So if I was you,' he says, pullin' on his feckin' pants, 'I'd reframe this whole thing in your mind. After all, wasn't I doin' you a favor, after all?'"

My cell rang, and I watched him as I pulled it from my pocket. He was saying, "I mean, it was fifteen of the best years of me life spent behind bars, but I don't regret a bit of it."

I said, "Yeah?"

It was the brigadier. "Harry, where are you?"

"I'm at Carlow East, on Lexington, drowning my sorrows."

"Are you drunk?"

"I keep trying, but I don't seem to be making it."

"I'll be there in five minutes."

"Is the colonel with you?"

There was a short pause, then, "You are drunk, Harry."

I sighed. "Okay, see you in five."

The colonel, Jane Harrison, right then, after two Guinness and four shots, was the only woman in the world capable of understanding me and making me happy. And it was down to me to cut through the crap and make her see that.

Maybe Sean was right. The mind was its own place and could make a hell of heaven. I took a good pull on the Guinness and chased it down with the shot. My mind had just turned to Claire, in Pinedale, and I was considering that she was also the only woman in the world capable of understanding me and making me happy, and it was down to me to cut through the crap and make her see that, when the brigadier climbed on the stool next to me and told Sean, "I'll have what he's having and give him another shot, would you?"

We took our drinks to a table, and he sat opposite me. I noticed there was rain on the shoulders of his coat.

"I have a job for you."

"I told you I hadn't made up my mind yet."

He gave a brief nod. He had gray eyes, and they were cold right then. It was an expression I had seen in him before, just before he shot somebody.

"Well," he said, without much feeling, "you can either make up your mind now or just do the job and make up your mind afterwards."

I blinked at him. He gave a small sigh.

"You know, Harry, perhaps you were misinformed on your way here. Life is shit, and it only gets worse. You have one major problem in life. Women want to sleep with you, but they don't want to marry you."

I felt a jolt of anger in my belly and muttered, "Thanks!"

He shook his head. "Don't think I am making little of it. I happen to know what that's like. But here's a couple of thoughts for you. One, it's better than it being the other way around..."

He paused for me to think about that, and I couldn't help smiling. "Fair point, sir."

"And you get more of what you focus on. So the longer you sit around feeling sorry for yourself, the worse the situation will become." He pointed at my drinks. "And keep this up much longer and they won't even want to sleep with you anymore." He raised his shot. "Cheers!"

We toasted and knocked them back. He put down the glass and leaned forward.

"The best way to shake these blues you're wallowing in is to see face to face just how hard it can get for people worse off than you."

I grunted. "Where?"

"At a lithium mine in Argentina, in the foothills of the Andes."

I frowned. "Who's down there?"

He sat back and took a deep breath, like he was thinking. "Well, that is sort of the point. We're not sure. We have reports that the mine is using slave labor. The reports are not reliable – at least, we are not sure whether they are reliable or not. If they are, then men, women, and children are being exploited as slaves in the mine and the processing plants."

"So this is not a hit. You want me to investigate."

"Initially, yes. If you find the reports are accurate, then you would identify the target or targets and execute the hits. We would also want you to shut down the mine."

"Shut it down?"

He raised an eyebrow. "Yes. We'd like to make it unattractive as an investment so that our own investors can move in and take it over."

I had no idea what a lithium mine would look like, or how you'd shut it down, but I could see the kids, half naked, hungry, probably beaten, and without thinking, I said, "Okay, have you made the arrangements? When do I go?"

"As soon as possible. You'll be a travel writer exploring Argentina and the Argentine Andes. That will give you some cover and a reason to snoop around. But be cautious because my guess is that security will be tight. The consequences for them if they are caught could be very severe. They'll be protecting themselves."

"So I just turn up and start asking questions about what the town has to offer...?"

"No, we've attached you to the magazine *Vagabond*. You will in essence be working for them, and we have asked them to approach the mayor of the village."

"What village?"

"Poman. It's about ninety miles from the nearest large town, Catamarca – thirty miles as the crow flies, but three times that climbing into the foothills of the Andes. So the approach we have made to the mayor is that you are writing about the Argentine Andes, and it might draw some tourism. We imagine that he will be courteous and accommodating but encourage you to explore farther north or farther south. You should at least have a week or two in which to investigate the mine."

"Where is the mine in relation to the village?"

"Three miles north. The exact coordinates will be in your file. The main access is from Highway 46, which lies about two miles to the east. However, that access will take you to a large barbed wire gate and fence protected by armed guards."

"I won't be going in that way."

"Your best approach is by night along a broad dirt track that leads from the village to a rear entrance. This is the route used by the villagers who work at the mine. Aside from that, I can tell you little. We have no intelligence regarding alarm systems, security, dogs..." He trailed off, shaking his head, then added, "This is why your mission is initially primarily reconnaissance."

"Okay, will I have any contact there?"

"I will be at Catamarca. I'll be staying at the American. When you need to report, you meet me there, and we will discuss the action to be taken. We have access to some ordnance in Argentina."

"I don't know what a lithium mine looks like. I don't know what I'll need to shut it down."

"You'll find that information in your brief. If that proves necessary, we will provide you with the hardware. Right now, what you need to focus on is whether there is in fact slavery going on there. If the answer to that is in the positive, then we need to know how bad it is. Is there torture involved? If so, who is being tortured, and how? Are people being murdered? In what numbers and again, how? Once we have these facts nailed down, we can start thinking about the steps to be taken."

"Okay." I nodded. "I'm in." And as I said it, I realized that it felt good.

———

THE FLIGHT from New York to Buenos Aires was over five thousand miles, and from there, I had to take another flight in an old prop-driven Fokker five hundred miles across Argentina into the foothills of the Andes. We finally touched down in Catamarca in the early afternoon. I collected my large rucksack, slung it in the back of my RAM 1500 rental, and set off along the imaginatively named Acceso al Aeropuerto toward their Highway 38, which would lead me, eventually, through the mountains up to the village of Poman.

The road was long and straight and ran through the center of a flat, featureless valley populated by low, scrubby trees I could not identify. The earth was a rusty red, and here and there, vast, circular fields had been plowed out: gigantic scars where the cycle of life had been industrialized to feed the human plague and the insatiable numbered accounts of the fattest, greediest parasites.

To my right, the Andes rose suddenly, a massive, dark blue

wall against the near-white sky. After fifteen minutes, I came to an intersection with a blue sign that told me this was Route 19, which lead me straight toward the mountains. Slowly and steadily, I began to climb as the sun slipped into bronzed afternoon and the shadows around me began to grow and stretch.

I climbed steadily through deep gorges and canyons where the steep sides of the hills crowded in over the road. The bends were tight hairpins, and the road was narrow, meaning every bend was also blind and forced me to go slowly, even though the traffic was minimal.

My GPS told me it would be a two-hour drive, but by the time I finally came out onto the arid highlands, an hour and three quarters had passed since I'd pulled out of the airport. Here at least the road was long and straight. I put my foot down and hurtled through the high desert closing on a hundred miles per hour. It was a landscape of desolation where what few trees there were had become gnarled by the summer heat and the frigid nights and winters.

Suddenly, as though I had driven through some quantum portal, the desolate desert threw up an orchard, and then another. I slowed. A garden appeared and a shaded path among old, Spanish houses with terracotta roofs and orange groves. Then, just as suddenly, I was entering a village with grim, narrow streets, dark houses with no windows, that had once been painted white, yellow, or salmon pink with lime wash but now were colored only with grime and neglect.

I slowed practically to a walking pace moving over the broken asphalt, among the cracked sidewalks and the dilapidated houses until I came to Jerónimo Luís de Cabrera Street. There, on my right, opposite the volunteer fire truck station, was a building that had probably been beige in the 1790s. It had stucco that had been picked out in white, probably around the same time, and a big hand-painted sign stuck to the wall claiming that the Pomanti Hotel had bedrooms, Wi-Fi, private bathrooms, and a thing called a yakuzi, which I guessed was not a Latin plural for a member of the Japanese underworld.

There were four doors. They were all painted yellow and white, and they were all closed. I parked the car in an area of wasteland just past the hostel, killed the engine, and walked to the middle door. It had seven flags hanging above it. None of them was the Stars and Stripes, and the only European one was Spanish. There was no bell, so I rapped with my knuckles and pushed.

The door juddered and swung open onto a small entrance hall with a gray tiled floor and a large arch onto an internal patio. There were a couple of wooden-framed armchairs that were modern and fashionable about the same time the Beatles had pudding basin haircuts, and there were a couple of dark, wooden doors, one on my right and one on my left. They had glass panels in them, but the one on my right had a printed sign stuck to the glass with sticking tape. It read *Oficina*. I took a wild guess and figured that meant office. So I stepped inside, knocked, and pushed through the door. There were two women there behind a melamine reception desk. One looked old enough to be Methuselah's grandmother. She had one tooth left in her lower jaw, and that looked even older than she did.

The other woman was in her early twenties and might have been the model for the clichéd Hollywood Latina, complete with black eyes and a sultry scowl. They were both staring at me. Mama Methuselah had her mouth sagging slightly, and her one tooth seemed to be pointing at me, like some weird kind of dowsing rod designed to seek out Americans. The other one had her head tilted forward and was giving me the treatment from under perfect eyebrows.

I smiled, but nothing happened. Sultry and ancient was the tone, and nothing was going to change that. "Habla ingles?"

Sultry said, "You are in Argentina. In Argentina, people espeakin' espanish."

"If I promise to learn, will you check my booking and show me my room?"

She sighed. "What is your name?"

"Bauer, Harry Bauer. I have a reservation."

She looked at a flat screen behind the desk and rattled at the keys on her keyboard. The action looked weirdly out of place in the setting. While she rattled, I looked up at the ceiling. It was exquisitely made of wooden beams that were probably more than two hundred years old.

"You are writer."

Something in her tone made me look at her. It wasn't a question. It was a bald statement, but I said, "Yes."

"I take you to your room."

"Thanks."

She came around the desk on shapely legs that made her hips swing, and I followed those legs and those hips across an internal patio with potted palms and up a wooden staircase to a galleried landing with evenly spaced heavy wooden doors in a white lime-washed wall. At the end, she unlocked one of those doors and went in ahead of me. I followed down a short passage. The floor was tiled in terracotta. There was a bathroom on my right, and then the room opened out. There was a big brass bed, and as I dumped my bag on it, she opened a set of tall, green, slatted French doors onto a small balcony that overlooked the ugly street below. Over the bed, there was a large, wooden fan like a propeller.

She stood framed in the open terrace door. The contrast made it hard to see the expression on her face. "What you are writing?"

"I'm a travel writer. I write about interesting, remote places."

"There is nothing interesting in Poman."

I gave my shoulders a small shrug. "Maybe there is and you just don't know about it."

"How long you are going to stay?"

"I don't know. If you are right and there is nothing interesting here, I'll leave in a week. If you're wrong, I'll stay longer."

She didn't move. She didn't react. After a moment, she said, "What is interesting?"

I crossed my arms and raised my shoulders high, like her question made thought, and therefore a bigger shrug, necessary.

"I don't know: music festivals, traditional carnivals, archeological remains..." I trailed off. "Most places have something. You're in the foothills of the Andes. That's interesting."

"There are no music festivals here, no carnival, no archeology."

I felt like telling her the woman downstairs with the tooth was an interesting archeological relic but pulled out my wallet instead and held out ten bucks.

"Thanks," I said. "If you think of anything that might be interesting for an American writer, let me know."

"We are all American, Mr. Bauer. You are North American, I am South American, but we are all American."

"Yeah," I said, "I know" and smiled on the side of my face where it doesn't look like a smile. She approached, took the ten North American dollars, brushed past me, and opened the door. "Oh," I said and stopped her. "I'm expecting a telephone call from your mayor. He thinks Poman is real interesting."

She waited for me to finish, with her eyes fixed on the terracotta tiles at her feet. When I was done, she left, closing the door behind her.

TWO

I SHOWERED AND SHAVED, AND BY THE TIME I WAS putting on a clean shirt, there was a tap at the door. When I opened it, Sultry was there leaning with her ass against the gallery balustrade.

"The mayor's office on the telephone for you."

I arched an eyebrow at her. "Can't you put it through to my room?"

"Is no workin' the telephone in your room."

"Right."

"They fixin' it."

By which I figured she meant they were fixing the bug. I nodded. "What's your name?"

"Carla Montoya."

She led me down to reception again where the tame zombie was still pointing at me with her gravestone tooth. I picked up the old bakelite receiver and said, "Hello? This is Harry Bauer."

I was surprised to hear a woman's voice on the other end. Contrary to what Colonel Jane Harris, the chef of operations at Odin believes, I am not a misogynist. I believe women are eminently well suited to any job that involves telling people what to do. I just don't expect them to be in those jobs in the foothills of the Andes.

And it turned out I was right. The pretty voice said, "Mr. Bauer, I am telephoning you on behalf of Mr. Nelson McCormack, the mayor of Poman. His English is not so good, but he would like to invite you to have luncheon with him, if you are free."

I smiled at the menacing tooth across the reception desk, and the bulging eyes that lay staring behind it. "That would be wonderful," I said.

"Will you be free in half an hour?"

"As soon as you like."

There was a smile in the voice when she said, "I'll be there in ten minutes."

I hung up and turned. Carla was leaning on the jamb of the open door, watching me. There were a lot of dark emotions swimming in her dark brown eyes, but the one that was most evident on the surface was judgment, judgment and her sister, condemnation. I smiled without feeling.

"Did something interesting just happen in Poman?"

Her lip curled, and she pushed off the jamb. "If something interesting happen in Poman, you don't see it and you don't hear it. It happen in the dark, at night."

I was torn between boredom and curiosity. So I made for the door, then paused and frowned. By that time, she was behind the desk, leaning on it with her elbows.

"Americans!" She said it like she was summing up everything that was wrong with fast food. "Makin' bombs, invisible airplanes, laser guns, everything to fight the Chinese and the Russians. Meantime the Chinese is investing, investing, investing, buying all the poor countries in the world. One belt, one road, and stupid America just watching, arguing about men in women's toilets and sports, while China becomin' bigger, more rich, more powerful."

I stared at her for a long moment, then gave my head a twitch.

"You don't make Poman sound boring. You make it sound interesting."

She crooked her index finger and rapped it on the counter. "Why America don't invest here? Make a partnership with Argentina! Build a factory for light! One F16 can make that factory and bring light and water to thousands of people!"

I returned to the desk and leaned on it, looking down at her. "Isn't that your government's job?"

"But they do nothing! They just give license the Chinese government. And they invest their money, no in makin' light; they invest their money in darkness. Things that happen at night, when doors and windows are closed and nobody is lookin'!"

I made a face of ironic disbelief and said, "Yeah, right. No music festivals, but a Fu Manchu conspiracy?"

I was about to return to my room and tell her to call me when the car arrived when there was a honk outside. A moment later, her cell pinged, and she gave me a look that said she'd like to skin me alive and eat my heart raw.

"Your paymaster is here, in the car outside."

I made a show of indignation and scowled at her. "I don't have a paymaster, sweetheart. I am freelance, independent. I work for me."

At the door, I stopped and turned back. "You have something to tell me, tell me. Cut out the snide comments and talk."

Outside, the midday sun was hot. The temperature was probably only in the nineties, but at that altitude, in the thin air, ninety can feel like a hundred and ten.

There was a Mercedes Maybach blocking the road outside and an attractive, well-dressed woman leaning against the passenger door watching me as I came out. She smiled and approached with her hand held out.

"Mr. Bauer? I am Rosario Fuentes, assistant to the mayor, Don Nelson McCormack. He has asked me to take you to Nacho's for a drink, and he will meet us there very soon."

I told her it sounded good, and she opened the door for me.

The smile we exchanged was perhaps a little friendlier than the occasion called for.

It was a short drive through dilapidated orchards and lots where half the houses seemed to be half built. The rule seemed to be half of the ground floor was finished, and the rest of the house was raw cement and concrete with gaping holes where the windows should be.

I told her, "I guess there was a property boom that didn't last long enough for the building boom that followed to get finished?"

She smiled. For a moment, I thought she wasn't going to answer, but then she said, "Economies in rural Argentina are very fragile. People do what they can. When times are good, they invest in their property. Sometimes the money runs out."

"It looks that way. What about you? Are you from Poman?"

Again the protracted silence, like she was calibrating her answer.

"My parents were from Poman. My father was the doctor. He did not agree with the idea of investing in property." She glanced at me. "He said there are many kinds of property. A prison is a property. Better to invest in a good lawyer than make your prison more comfortable."

"Smart guy. So what did he do? He sent you to college to study law in Catamarca?"

The contraction on her face was almost imperceptible. "He sent me to study law in Buenos Aires."

"How old were you?"

She looked like she didn't know whether to be affronted or simply surprised. Instead of making up her mind, she said, "We are here."

We pulled in to a crescent drive off the road. The building was modern – or had been in the '50s – rectilinear white boxes stacked on top of each other, with lots of plate glass. Outside, there were tables made of steel tubing and plastic with their corresponding chairs. She killed the engine, and we climbed out.

Before we got to the door, a guy I took to be the owner came stumbling out, reaching for her with both hands and grinning too hard. As he drew closer, he didn't touch her. Her face said that wasn't allowed. Instead, he gestured toward the door and bowed. He kept saying, "Doña Rosario" and mumbling in Spanish.

She ignored him, and I followed her inside. There was a small dining room with a dozen tables made of melamine and steel tubing and a bar that ran down the right hand side. Rosario crossed the room and pushed through a door that said *PRIVADO*. I followed. The swing of her hips made that easy. She pushed through a second door, and we were out on a flagged patio with an exotic garden and a fountain that made a good pretence of being ancient and possibly Greek.

There were two steel tubing tables that had been pushed together and covered in a white linen tablecloth. They were set with the restaurant's best stainless steel and lead-free crystal.

She took a seat with her back to the yard and the fountain, and I sat opposite her. The door opened, and the owner came out, still bowing. She rattled something at him in Spanish. I head something about martini, and then she looked a question at me. I said, "Scotch, on the rocks."

When he'd gone, I said, "I hope my question didn't offend you."

She shrugged and forced a smile. "Why should it offend me?"

I returned the smile. "I can't imagine." I gestured at her with an open hand. "You are obviously a very elegant, sophisticated, cultured woman. That doesn't happen in four or five years of college while you're burning the midnight oil trying to memorize contract law."

She arched a very elegant eyebrow. "Wow."

I raised my shoulders an eighth of an inch. "The magazine pays me a lot because I am very observant."

"Papa sent me to a private boarding school in Buenos Aires, then I went to university there."

I grinned. "I could have told you that. What I am wondering is how the mayor of Poman can afford you."

"You are becoming impertinent, Mr. Bauer." She said it like she didn't really mind.

"I'm here looking for what's interesting. Right now, the most interesting thing I have found in Poman is you. And I am wondering why the mayor of a tiny village in the foothills of the Andes, where the hotel hasn't even got a bar, has an assistant with a degree in law from the best university in Argentina and enough style and intelligence to be on the board of any of Argentina's multinationals."

She was quiet for a long moment, trying to read my face. Finally she said, "How do you know I have a degree in law?"

"It's written on your forehead and in the way you walk. I'd go so far as to say you did a masters at an American university. You walk like a United States defense attorney. But I might be wrong, and then I'd lose my reputation and my credibility."

She blinked slowly three times before saying, "Columbia. If I didn't know it was impossible, I'd say you'd been checking up on me."

I gave a small laugh. "But then I'd know the answer to my question, wouldn't I? I am just good at guessing. Let's face it, what's a girl like you doing in a place like this?"

The door opened, and a waiter stepped out with a tray bearing a martini and a Scotch on the rocks. When he'd gone, we toasted and she sipped. As she set down her glass, she said, "The mayor of Poman is my uncle. This is a very small town, and most people are related. A year ago, the LitArg corporation was founded for the purpose of finding and exploiting lithium mines in South America. They believe this is the oil of tomorrow, and Argentina will be the Saudi Arabia of the future."

"Makes sense, but how does that affect you?"

"The LitArg prospectors found a very large lithium mine outside Poman, and my uncle found he was out of his depth negotiating with these high-powered lawyers. So he asked me to come and help." She gave a small shrug. "In Argentina, family counts."

I made an appreciative face. "So that's good news for Poman, right?"

She didn't answer. She just sipped her drink. Maybe she thought the question was rhetorical. So I added, "Well, I am extremely flattered that your uncle dragged you away from your meetings with LitArg to entertain me, a humble hack from a travel rag."

"How many meetings do you think we have a month, Mr. Bauer? Once the contracts are settled, there is very little contact, as you well know. In fact, I will be going back to Buenos Aires in another week or so. I am sure you are also aware that for my uncle, a visit from a journalist representing a magazine – not a rag, as you say – such as *Vagabond*, which is read all over the world, could be an important boost for tourism. Are all travel journalists as suspicious as you, Mr. Bauer?"

I laughed. "I am not suspicious, Rosario, and please call me Harry. Maybe I am just flirting with you. Are you married?"

"My goodness! You don't waste time, do you?"

"Apparently I only have a week."

She gave a small sigh. "I am married, Mr. Bauer – Harry – to my job and to my family."

"Package deal, huh?"

"That is the way it is in Latin America. Do you think this is an appropriate conversation for"—she gestured at me with an open hand—"a journalist and a representative of local government?"

I smiled. "Not really, Rosario. But as you said, I am a journalist, and journalists are not supposed to be appropriate. We are the fourth estate. It's our job to be inappropriate."

Her face said she was feeling skeptical. "The fourth estate? Before the French revolution, in France, the church was the first estate, the aristocracy was the second, and the commoners were the third. Then the printing press came along, and problematic thinkers and idealists started printing leaflets, spreading seditious ideas. It was Edmund Burk who called you the fourth estate, and if I am not mistaken, he was mocking you."

I arched an eyebrow at her over my whiskey. "Just because I mockingly call you the desirable lady across the table, it doesn't mean you are *not* the desirable lady across the table."

She didn't smile, but her cheeks did color. "Please, Mr. Bauer, you have to stop this."

There were voices outside. The door opened, and a small crowd of men spilled through. At a quick estimate, I calculated there were about twice as many as would fit at the table. The one at the center was in his late sixties in an expensive off-the-peg suit. His hair and his skin said he'd spent a lot of hours recently in a hair salon and a beauty parlor having the last sixty years of toiling in unforgiving Andean fields cleaned out of his skin and his hair with expensive lotions and massages. He probably didn't know where Paris was, but he knew that was where his lotions came from.

I stood.

Two guys went and stood on the other side of the door. Two stood on this side of the door, and two more went and stood out in the yard. The sixty-plus guy in the expensive suit and hair grinned and held out his hand. "Señor Bauer," he said with a little sing-song. "Es un gran placer darle la bienvenida a este, nuestro humilde pueblo."

He glanced at Rosario as I took his hand and shook it.

"Mr. Nelson McCormack says it is his pleasure to welcome you to this, our humble village."

I gave his hand a good squeeze. "Please tell him it is an honor for me to be here." She translated, and I added, "So far I have found it fascinating and surprising, and I am anxious to discover everything there is to know about it."

He nodded and listened as she translated, with his mouth slightly open. Then he grinned at me and nodded more vigorously. We all sat, and he started giving elaborate instructions to the waiter.

THREE

THE WINE WAS FROM CATAMARCA AND NOT BAD, the steaks were also local and probably the best I had ever eaten. The conversation was labored and tedious. He would ramble at length to Rosario, while I took my time savoring the steak, and then she would relay to me.

"He says, what has Poman to offer a visitor? It has a great deal to offer -"

At this point, he would throw his hands over his head and say, "Mucho! Mucho!"

"Our traditional cuisine is, as you can see for yourself, exceptional. The wine is from lower down in the valley, in Catamarca, and the beef farms are to the south. Also to the south, we have magnificent hunting; especially the red stag is a magnificent trophy."

She paused while he spoke, then turned to me.

"Of course there is much skiing in Neuquen, Rio Negro, and Chubut provinces, in the south. But we hope, with infrastructure and investment, we can make maybe ski lodges in the west, higher in the mountains."

I interrupted. "That's nice, but what about the village of Poman? What plans have you for the town?"

She translated. I finished my steak and settled back with my wine while they spoke. Eventually she turned to me and smiled.

"Excuse me. He is saying that our main priority is to try to attract investment to the area. If we can do this, then perhaps people in the village, who are very hard-working good people, will maybe invest in making better hotels, maybe we can find money to make the village more attractive and bring tourists. So he is encouraging you to investigate our beautiful countryside to the south and to the east, the vineyards, the great cattle ranches, the hunting, the wonderful wildlife, and encourage tourism to come."

I nodded and sipped. "Oh sure, and the cuisine. That is a wonderful steak and great wine. What's to the north and the west?"

She translated, and they both did a lot of shrugging and flinging their hands around.

"North and west right now is nothing, dangerous areas because they are so remote, very high up with no oxygen, wild animals, wolves, cougar, snakes, scorpions." She laughed. "Even sometimes some bandits. It is a good place to hide."

"Wow!" I laughed. "So stay clear of north and west, but south and east is good, to encourage tourists instead of bandits."

She translated, and we all laughed. Just after that, he stood and addressed me directly in Spanish. When he was done, we both looked at Rosario.

"He says it has been a pleasure to meet you, and he hopes that he will have the honor of your company again before you leave. Anything you need, do not hesitate to contact his office or me."

"Tell him I have no immediate plans to leave, and I would love to see him again soon, after I have done some exploring, to ask him some questions for my articles."

She translated, and there was a lot of amiable nodding and hand-shaking. Then he and his six bodyguards trooped out to his car. When he was gone, she took hold of her purse and tilted her head on one side.

"Is there anything else you need, Mr. Bauer?"

I nodded slowly a few times. "Nothing you can give me right now," I said. "It would have been nice to finish my wine and have a chat. Maybe another day, when you stop calling me Mr. Bauer and start calling me Harry."

"I am sorry if I have offended you."

"You haven't offended me, Rosario. Or should I call you Ms. Fuentes? But I would like you to chill and relax and help me get to know the area. Is that a problem?"

"Of course not. Anything you need."

As she said it, she reached in her purse and pulled out a card, which she handed to me. I sighed, took it, laughed, and shook my head all at the same time. "Okay, I give up. Let me get some sleep after the flight. I'll spend the next few days exploring south, east, north, and west, and then I'll come to you with a list of questions. Tell your boss thanks for lunch."

"I will drive you back."

It was a three- or four-minute drive, but the awkward silence made it seem longer. She pulled up outside the hotel, and as I opened the door, she said, "I was not exaggerating about the dangers north and west. You are from New York. You do not understand what real wilderness is like. People die out there. Even local people. Please, stay south and east. Or if you go north and west, tell me, so that I know where you are if you get into trouble."

I nodded. "Thanks."

I watched her pull away up the road toward city hall, then went inside, wondering if Carla Montoya, the Latina firebrand, would still be at reception, or if it would just be Tomb Tooth. As it turned out, it was neither of them. So I went up to my room. It had been a long flight from New York, and I had been about twenty-four hours without sleep. So I fell on the bed and slipped rapidly into oblivion.

I awoke four hours later to the sound of dusk turning to evening. It's a time of day that has its own sounds, especially in remote Latin villages. They are the sounds, oddly muffled by the dying light, of people coming home, dads parking their cars, greeting their families, moms calling their kids in for dinner and having a last gossip with the neighbor before closing out the night.

I sat up, stripped, and went to the bathroom, where I stood under the cold jets from the shower for five minutes. Then I dressed, opened my leather bag, and took my Sig Sauer P226 and my Fairbairn and Sykes from the sealed compartment in the base. Whatever the nerds at Cobra had done to it, the contents were invisible to the scanning equipment at airports.

I slipped the Sig in its holster under my arm, pulled on a linen jacket, and strapped the knife to my calf. Then I went downstairs. There was no one in reception, but as I stepped through the door out into the street, I heard a footfall behind me and turned. It was Carla.

"Where you are going this time of night?"

I laughed. "What are you, my mother?" She didn't share the laugh. There was no expression on her face, but her eyes were like drills. I took a couple of steps back toward her. "You have a restaurant or a bar in your hostel?"

"You know we haven't."

"So I'm going out to get dinner."

"At six o'clock? When you have your lunch at two?"

"That's a lot of observing you're doing there, Carla. What's your problem?"

She didn't answer. She jerked her chin at my left shoulder. "You need to take this to have dinner at Nacho's? Nobody gonna try an' shoot you in Nacho's."

I took a moment to frown at her. The only movement she made was to lean her shoulder against the jamb and wait for my answer. I was aware I had a situation, but I'd be damned if I knew what that situation was.

"Do you have a reason for being this observant?"

"You got a reason for carrying a gun?"

"If I answer your question, will you answer mine?"

"Try me."

"I'm an American journalist traveling in the most remote parts of Latin America. Maybe you don't know this, but guys from the United States are not the most popular people in this part of the world." I smiled without much humor. "Mexico, Guatemala, El Salvador, Panama, Colombia, Venezuela, Brazil..." I gave a small shrug. "You get into the habit of carrying protection."

"You expect me to believe this?"

"I don't care whether you believe it or not. Now it's your turn. Why the interest? Why do you care at what time I have dinner and whether I carry a gun?"

She pushed off the jamb and went to turn. I stopped her.

"I'm going to take a drive around the outskirts of town to see if I can spot any wildlife. You want to come?"

She stood and stared at me for a long moment. Then she shook her head.

"No. Be careful. There are dangerous animals out at night."

She went inside and closed the door. I stood a moment thinking, then made my way to my car.

I turned it around and went back out the way I'd come into town. Dusk was turning from grainy to evening, the lights were coming on in the houses, and the sky was turning from splashes of crimson and violet to turquoise and aquamarine. I followed the glow of my headlights past the crescent drive into Nacho's and out into the darkness of the wilderness. I drove slowly for a couple of miles, then killed the lights and came off onto a dirt track on my right. There I killed the engine and climbed out.

There was no moon, but there was a glow on the eastern horizon. Above, the sky was crystal clear in the thin air, and the Milky Way, almost invisible in most of the northern hemisphere, here was a blaze of silver light across the vast dome.

I climbed into the flatbed and stood looking in all directions. It was dark, flat shrubland as far as the eye could see, except to the north and the west where the Andes rose in a jagged black wall against the sky.

I turned to the north and east again, and as my eyes adjusted, I began to realize that the glow I had attributed to the rising moon was not the moon at all. There was a slight rise in the ground before it dipped. Thinking back to the map of the area I had studied on the plane, that dip went down to a river that came down out of the mountains. I wondered why a river would be giving off light at night.

I jumped down and climbed back in the cab. I left the lights off, kept my feet off the pedals, and rolled along the track at ten miles an hour. After three or four minutes, I came to a kind of oblong water reservoir on my right, surrounded by small, stunted trees. I pushed on another hundred yards, and the ground fell away ahead of me. I braked and killed the engine.

It was a little over half a mile away. At first glance, it looked like a football field illuminated by spotlights. But as I looked closer, I could see it was a mine. Or, to be more precise, it was the processing plant for a mine.

I took a small pair of high-powered binoculars I had in the glove compartment and climbed back onto the bed. It was hard to tell exactly at that distance, but as I watched, I could make out the trucks bringing in the ore and dumping it into the mills. I thought I could make out the granulators too, where the lithium is made into granules with the hydride and dolomite reagents. I could see what I assumed to be the fluidized beds and the kilns where the lithium is dried at close to two thousand degrees before the final concentration process.

I sat a while, thinking about trying to get closer and get a good look at the workers. But as I sat there, I could see the steady flow of patrol trucks moving around the perimeter of the plant. I could also see trucks and Jeeps moving around inside and wondered why you would need such tight security at a remote lithium mine and processing plant. It was a rhetorical wondering.

I figured the processing plant was in the region of a hundred and fifty acres. The mine itself was impossible to tell. The spotlights of the plant cast everything behind it into total blackness, but with a processing plant of that size, apparently working twenty-four hours, you could be looking at anything over four thousand acres.

That was a lot of workforce. Where were they getting the workers from?

I jumped down and pulled myself into the cab, then sat drumming my fists on the steering wheel. I needed to come back and have a look in daylight. But the land was flat for miles, the trees were all stunted and gave no cover and, to make matters worse, because the processing plant was in a slight hollow, it meant anyone observing the damned place would be raised up into full view.

It was a problem that needed some thought.

I was about to shove the key in the ignition when the high whine of a Jeep reached me through the open window. I paused and looked and saw two headlights approaching, jerking and bumping across the uneven terrain and the small, gnarled bushes. I slipped the fighting knife from my boot and slipped it into my jacket sleeve, then opened the door and swung down from the cab.

I squinted into the glare of the approaching lights, shielding my eyes with my raised right hand. They ground to a halt six or eight feet away, and two indistinct figures moved behind the light, shouting in Spanish.

I said, "No hablo español. Amigo invitado Alcalde Nelson McCormack."

I told them I didn't speak Spanish, but I was a friend of the mayor's. I was interested to see how they'd react. It made them pause. Then they moved out in front of the lights and came and stood up close, looking up at me. It's hard to intimidate a guy if you have to look up at him, but they did their best. They were hard. If they had ever known compassion, it had shriveled and died inside them. Their eyes said they were accustomed to killing, and they were weighing whether to kill me now.

The one on my left had his hand on the butt of a holstered revolver. The one on my right had an assault rifle slung over his shoulder. The guy with the sidearm jerked his chin at me.

"How you know the alcalde?"

He had languages. He was obviously the intellectual of the outfit.

"I had lunch with him today," I said, "Comer, comer," and I moved my hands up and down toward my mouth like I was eating. That made them frown, but by then, it was too late because I had slipped the Fairbairn and Sykes from my sleeve and driven it through Sidearm's esophagus and out through his vertebrae.

The guy with the rifle was still gaping when I broke his nose with my elbow, slipped the rifle from his shoulder, and smashed the butt into the side of his knee. He fell to the ground whimpering. I pulled my knife from Sidearm's neck and dropped my right knee on the guy with the rifle's chest. He was sobbing and babbling in Spanish and kept trying to reach for his knee.

"You speak English? Habla ingles?"

He was shaking his head, and his voice was getting loud. I put my finger to my lips, then pointed down to the processing plant. "Niños? Trabajar niños?" I tried to think of slaves in Spanish. "Slavos?"

I knew it wasn't that, but it was close enough. He nodded, still sobbing. "Esclavos, si. Niños esclavos trabajan allí. Por favor, por piedad, no me mate. Yo le informo."

I guess it wasn't his lucky day. He'd just told me there were child slaves working there, and if I didn't kill him, he would inform on them. If I'd been a real journalist, he'd be my ticket to a Pulitzer, and I'd be all about keeping him alive.

But I was not a real journalist, and I had no interest in earning a Pulitzer. He also asked me for pity. But when it comes to men who collaborate in enslaving children and threaten them with guns, pity is something I find I have in short supply.

I arched an eyebrow at him and said, "Piedad?"

Then I cut through his aorta and his carotid artery. He bled out in seconds and, I thought to myself, if there is anything in the Buddhist idea that our dying thought conditions our next life, this son of a bitch died questioning whether he had a right to compassion. And that was as close as he was going to get to pity from me.

I killed the lights on the Jeep, wiped my prints off the rifle, and made my way back to the hotel.

FOUR

I LEFT THE TRUCK PARKED OUT FRONT AND WENT IN TO
reception. I had a theory which I wanted to put to the test. I
found Carla sitting behind the reception desk looking at her
computer screen. She closed the screen and looked up. There was
defiance in her eyes, like I was about to ask her who Spartacus was.

"You are back so soon?"

I held her eye for a moment. "Are you under the impression
that I went out?" She frowned. "Do you think that I came down
earlier and went out in my truck, saying I was going to look for
wildlife?" The frown stayed in place, but I could almost hear her
brain at work. I shook my head. "That would be ridiculous. It was
too early for dinner, and there would be no wildlife till later in the
night. I have been up in my room, and I have come down just
now to go and have dinner at Nacho's."

The frown cleared, and she squared her shoulders. "Are you
threaten me?"

"No. What I am telling you is that whatever you may hear in
the next few hours, I came in from lunch, went to my room, and
have just come down now. And now I am going to go and have
dinner at Nacho's."

"I am not afraid of you, Mr. Bauer."

"Good." I leaned across the counter and stared hard into her eyes. "Because the people you need to be scared of, Carla, are the sons of bitches who enslave children and make them work in mines. I think you have a big conscience. So you do whatever your conscience tells you to do. I am telling you, I was in my room sleeping until now. And now I am going to have dinner."

I walked out, got in my truck, and drove down toward Nacho's. I had taken a risk, but I figured it was a small one. I needed an ally right then, and two got you twenty I could count on Carla if I was up against the mine.

I was also pretty sure she knew something, and when she heard that two guards at the mine had been killed, she might just feel inclined to confide in me.

I pulled up outside the restaurant. It was bright and crowded in the balmy night. I sat biting my lip and thinking for a moment, then I pulled my cell, found Rosario's number, and dialed.

It rang three times before she answered.

"Mr. Bauer, how can I help you?"

"You can have dinner with me."

A sigh. A sigh that would have put any guy off who actually gave a damn whether she liked him. "Mr. Bauer, I am about to sit down to dinner with..."

"Me too. I am about to sit down to dinner with nobody. And I couldn't help thinking, after you left, that the Andes rise and expand to the north and the west. Surely as you rise toward Ojos del Salado and el Peñón, the potential for world class ski resorts must be enormous. Finding investment would not be hard—"

"Mr. Bauer!

It is late..."

"I was thinking of driving out that way tomorrow. Maybe you could join me and I could explain to you the potential -"

She cut me short again. "You are at Nacho's?"

"Yes."

"I'll be there in ten minutes." She didn't sound like she was going on a date with her high school heartthrob. I smiled and said, "Super," but she'd already hung up.

I found a table on the terrace and told the waiter, "Whiskey, no hielo."

"No ice? Coca Cola? Seven Up?"

I guess my face told him everything he needed to know because he nodded and smiled like his life depended on it. Then I told him, "And martini for Señorita Rosario Fuentes."

"With vodka ice and lemon?"

"Is that how she always has it?"

"Si, yes."

"Then go do it."

He went away. Five minutes later, he came back with the drinks as Rosario was climbing out of her car. I stood to greet her as she approached. She nodded at me and sat without saying anything. She repressed a sigh as she looked at the martini.

"Vodka, ice, and lemon," I said. "The way you always have it."

"I had to cancel dinner with my uncle."

"I once had to cancel dinner with Kate Winslet." She frowned at me hard. "She was real busy filming, and I was in Afghanistan. So we had to call it off."

There was a moment of stillness. I watched her. She said, "Afghanistan..."

"I'm a reporter, remember?"

"A travel reporter, for *Vagabond*."

"Yeah, well, you know," I laughed. "Taking photographs of bits of people gets tiring. I thought I'd go for something a bit cozier. And you'd be surprised how well paid travel writing can be. You find a place everybody wants to know about, and the money just keeps rolling in."

If there was a prize for ambiguous smiles, I would have aced it right then. Her own expression shifted, from impatience to resignation. From there, it shifted again pretty quickly to an amused smile.

"All right, Mr. Bauer."

"Harry."

"Very well, Harry, why don't you tell me what this is about and what you want?"

"As a man or as a journalist?"

"Is there a difference?"

"Sure. As a journalist, I want to know the truth. As a man, like all men, I want power, money, and sex."

She closed her eyes and sighed. She was struggling. "What truth, *Mr. Bauer?*"

"Harry. What's to the north and west? You and the mayor fed me a lot of horseshit today. Go south and east, fascinating cattle ranches, great hunting. But don't go north and west, there be dragons! Come on, I was not born yesterday. What have you got going on northwest of here? I don't have to write about it. Everything can be negotiated. But I do need to know."

She shook her head. "You don't need to know."

"So there *is* something going on."

"Mr. Bauer. You need to pull back or you can find yourself in very serious trouble. Things happen in South America that you do not understand. People pry and people get killed."

"Is this supposed to stop my curiosity? Send me away and I'll hire a plane and fly over the area with a whole battery of cameras. What's going on here, Rosario? What could possibly be happening that is worth killing an international journalist over? Come on!"

There was a soft breeze that moved her hair. It was scented with jasmine and something sweet I didn't recognize.

"So now you are telling me you were a war correspondent, but you behave more like an investigative journalist. Whom do you really work for, Harry?"

"Who do I work for, or who do I sell to? I work for me, and I sell to the highest bidder. *Vagabond* provides my bread and butter. But a man like me has a lot to forget, and that takes a lot of booze and a lot of high living. So *Vagabond* will get to hear all about the cattle ranches and the hunting. Who gets to hear about the northwest foothills of the Andes? Well, that's kind of up to you."

"Are you trying to blackmail me?"

"Blackmail is an unwarranted demand backed by threats. If what you have north and west of here were legal and legitimate, Rosario, I don't think you'd have any trouble letting me see it. So if what you have going on out there is not strictly legitimate, I don't see how my demand can be unwarranted. Do you?"

I called the waiter and asked for two more drinks and a couple of menus. Around us, people were relaxing and getting noisy. I sipped my whiskey. Rosario had been watching her drink like she thought it might make a break for it. Now she took a hold of it and raised it halfway to her mouth.

"You are a brave man, Harry. Maybe stupid. After what I have told you, you must realize that your life is at risk."

I smiled. "Only if you and your people are even stupider than I am. And you may be lots of things, Rosario, but you are not stupid. You know by now that I know my business and I have experience in what I do. You know that if I am reporting from remote parts of the world, I have access to sophisticated electronic equipment. So you also know that I am going to take out insurance before I invite you to dinner for a chat. So no, I don't think I am at risk right now." I leaned forward with my elbows on the table, fixed her eyes, and smiled the kind of smile that doesn't bring sweet dreams.

"But you're right about one thing," I said. "I am brave and bold, and one more thing, Rosario. I am very, very dangerous. So if you are smart, you will take me seriously."

I thought she might get up and leave. I thought she might call someone to come and take me away and shoot me. She did neither. She looked away and struggled to repress a smile. Then she picked up her menu and started reading it. As she read, she said, "You are a very interesting man, Harry."

"That's what the midwife told my mother when I was born. Only she said specimen, not man."

"I will ask you again, what do you want?" I drew a breath, but she raised her big black eyes and smiled. "I already know what you want as a man, Harry. What do you want as a meddlesome reporter?"

The breeze caught her hair again, and her eyes were telling me there was everything to play for, and for a moment I thought her dark hair and her smooth, dark skin might be a good place to go and forget for a few hours.

"I want to know what lies north and west. Maybe you could tell me over a nightcap, after dinner."

"It's not up to me. I will have to check." She picked up her menu again. "But that doesn't mean I am saying no to the nightcap after dinner."

We ordered our food and wine, and over dinner we discussed Trump and Biden, Prince Harry and Meghan, the risks of artificial intelligence and the curious, unexplained greening effect of CO_2. We even discussed the relative values of the Roman legal system as compared with the Anglo-Saxon system. From there, we moved on to whether Buddhism was a religion or a subjective, existentialist philosophy, and I began to feel maybe I was out of my depth.

Things we did not discuss were journalism, blackmail, or the northwest area of the Catamarca Andes.

When the waiter had cleared our plates, I asked her, "Well, what about that nightcap?"

She held my eye with a steady gaze and said, "I'd like that very much. You should come to my place. I am sure it is more comfortable than that awful hotel." I can't deny I was feeling a warm glow in my belly. But then she said, "But not tonight, Harry. I need to make some important phone calls. You have really complicated matters. But I will call you later, or in the morning, to let you know what they say."

"Who's they?"

"That is something I will tell you tomorrow, or later tonight. Until what time can I call you?"

I shrugged and shook my head. "Anytime."

"Then we'll talk later. And after that, we'll have that nightcap."

I paid the check and walked her to her dark Audi. She gave me a real soft kiss on the cheek and drove away into the night. I climbed into my RAM and drove slowly back to my hotel, mulling over her reactions to both my advances. She had said I was at risk, but I was pretty sure they would want to know how much of a risk I would be to them – both dead and alive – before they took any action. So two got you twenty Rosario would be dispatched, pump in hand, to see what she could get out of me. That was a prospect I found surprisingly appealing.

On the other hand, one thing her reaction to my advances did seem to confirm beyond any reasonable doubt was that some kind of illegal operation was going down on a big scale. The mine was there, in the northwest, and they wanted it kept quiet. From what the guy with the rifle had said, there were child slaves there. So –

So nothing. The guy with the rifle and I had a big language and communication problem. He was terrified and would almost certainly have said anything to appease me. And as far as Rosario and her contacts were concerned, they could be using the mine as a cover for cultivating cocaine. It was unlikely, but what I had was not proof. And what I needed before I put on my executioner's robes was proof.

My last thought as I pulled into the wasteland at the back of the hotel was about how deeply Rosario was involved. If they were using child slaves, would the execution order extend to her? The brigadier had said I would have discretion.

I didn't want discretion. I wasn't sure I could be objective. If it came to it, I would have to talk to the brigadier and let him make the decision.

I swung down from the cab, locked the vehicle, and walked into the bright warmth of the hotel. There was no one on reception, so I made my way up to my room at the end of the galleried landing overlooking the central patio. I took a moment and looked down at the mass of bright red and purple flowers, ferns and palms in the terracotta pots. A warm, sweet smell rose on the evening air. I checked my watch. It was fifteen minutes after midnight. I let myself in my room and had a cold shower, then went and fell on the bed without drying myself.

I managed to doze fitfully. I awoke several times. The first time and the second I could hear people laughing and singing, revelers on their way home. The third time it was darker, like there were lights missing in the streets. I could hear trucks revving, and there was a knocking on my door. I sat up, unsure whether I had dreamed it, but it came again, soft, not loud. I looked at my watch. It was three a.m.

I rose and opened the door. The lights in the patio were off, but there was a moon, and I found myself squinting down at Carla, the firebrand from reception. A chill breeze made me shudder. She didn't look mad or as if she wanted to accuse me of imperialism or colonialism. I said, "Carla?"

"They find two dead men," she said. "You killed them."

FIVE

I SIGHED AND RAN MY FINGERS THROUGH MY HAIR.

"You better come inside."

"You are going to kill me?"

I gave her the kind of look you give a frog that asks you what coitus means. "*What? No!*"

I stood back, and she asked, "Are you going to rape me?"

"No! Will you get inside! I am not going to do anything to you." I gestured toward the room and said, "Sit."

She moved into the room and stood staring at the bed. "You should cover yourself, not sleep on top. You will catch cold."

I looked at her from the bathroom door, feeling slight brain-ache. "Thanks. Make yourself comfortable."

I stuck my head in the sink and dowsed it with cold water. I toweled my face and head, and as I removed the towel and opened my eyes, I saw her standing in the doorway holding two tooth mugs.

"I bring some whiskey," she said. "So that we can talk."

I was going to tell her coffee might have been a better plan. Instead I said, "Good thinking."

We left the lights off so as not to draw attention to my room. She sat in the chair by the balcony with the dim moonlight lying across her face, giving her skin an almost blue tint. I sat on the end of the bed and took a pull on the whiskey.

"What happened?" I said.

"The sergeant of the police he is come here. He is want to know if you are going out this evening?"

"If I went out."

She nodded. "Yes, if you are went out before. I remember what you say to me. So I tell him no, you have been in your room until maybe nine. Like you say."

"Thank you."

"You kill them."

I took another pull on my whiskey and watched her in her chair while I savored it. Instead of answering her, I asked, "Who were they?"

Her face contracted, and there was hatred in her dark eyes.

"Mercenarios!" She hissed it like the word was poisonous. "They are employ by Aquanecra Security Corporation, an American private security agency. So when American government don't want blood on its hands, they are call Aquanecra Security Corporation, so they can say, 'Oh, is not us!'"

"Wait, slow down. Try and stay on track, Carla. The guys who died were employed by an American security agency?"

"Yes!" She said it like it was my fault. "Aquanecra Security Corporation! They move here when the mine is open it makes one year."

"A year ago."

"Yes. You kill them."

"Why do you keep saying that?"

She didn't answer right away. We sat looking at each other in the dark, with the moonlight lying across the lower part of her face and her body. Her eyes were deep shadows, but I could feel her stare, like she was a surgeon opening me up to look inside.

"Because you have the eyes of a killer."

"I am a reporter."

"You are a liar."

"Thanks."

"You tell lies, you are a liar."

"Fine. What do you know about this place – the mine?"

She turned and looked out of the open balcony, past the tall French shutters. Her voice was quiet, like she was talking to herself.

"At first,

we were all happy. They say it will bring a lot of jobs. This is the beginning of a new life, green energy, good for the planet, and it will bring work and prosperity to this part of Argentina." She looked down at her glass, but she didn't drink. "At first, when they are building the place, it was good. There were jobs, but not enough people here for all the work. So they have to bring people from other towns. But many of them have a problem with altitude sickness, and the owners of the mine are in a hurry. They need get the mine and the processing plant working fast."

She trailed off. I said, "So what happened?"

"The was a change of policy." She turned and looked straight at me. "A change of policy," she said again. "The workers from the lowlands go back. They will use only mountain people. People who are use to the altitude. But they will live at the mine for one month, working every day. Then they have two weeks rest. Then back to the mine for a month. Then two weeks rest. And they take people from every town. They promise they are going to pay fantastic wages.

"And soon the workers are no coming home for two weeks. At first they tell, 'Oh, they want do overtime because they makin' so much money!' Then they say, 'Oh, they left the mine. We are no responsible. Maybe they go to Buenos Aires to spend all their money. Is your personal, matrimonial problem.'"

She went quiet. I waited. Outside, it was quiet. Far off, some bird cried out. She took a first sip from her whiskey and shuddered.

"What is your name?"

"Harry."

"That is your real name?"

"Yes."

"Maybe we are going to die. When I die I want to know your real name."

"My real name is Harry."

"Harry, have you seen any children in Poman?"

The obviousness of the question shook me. I thought back to when I drove in to town, I thought about lunch with the mayor, about dinner that night.

"No."

"The population of this town is small, so there are not many children. But the children that were here are at the mine."

I scowled. "How do you know? Why hasn't it been reported to the authorities?"

"I know because a bus come to the village, to the school, and all the children are put on the bus and take to the mine. This is a special service the mine do for us. They have make a school at the mine, where they have the best teachers, and anyone who work at the mine have their children educated at the mine school. My daughter, Lucia, is now at the mine."

"But surely you can report it to -"

"To who? The mayor? The chief of police? I go and talk to them. They tell me very clear. If I want their help, I must sleep with them. If I go to the authorities in Catamarca, it will be useless, and also my daughter will have bad accident at the mine. If I want see my child again, I shut up and wait. And if I want her to come home soon from the mine and stay at home, then I must pay."

"Pay..."

"Yes, this morning I was preparing my bag to go and stay the night with the mayor. When you came, I think maybe I will wait."

"You did right," I said quietly. "What about the school authorities? The principal, the teachers...?"

"The director of the school was furious. She complains to the mayor and to the directors of the mine. She tells them she is going to Catamarca to the delegation of education there, and if they will not listen, then she is going to Buenos Aires. She got in her car one month ago, and we have never heard again from her. Her telephone is disconnected. Her email is canceled. She does not exist."

I shook my head, frowning. "I don't understand. Last night I had dinner with Rosario Fuentes at Nacho's. There were people there dining, drinking, laughing. Do these people really believe—"

She cut me short. "What did they look like?"

"What?"

"These people, what did they look like? Did they have callused hands? Was their skin dried by the desert air? Were their clothes the clothes of poor peasants who live from what they can get from the poor soil at this altitude?"

I drained my glass and rubbed my face. "No, they weren't like that. They were managerial staff at the mine."

"Those are the people who eat and drink at Nacho's."

"You are certain about this?"

"Can you explain to me where is my daughter?"

I sighed and spoke half to myself. "You need to go to your room and you need to stay there. I'll wash these glasses and dry them thoroughly. Leave the bottle with me. I'll wipe your prints off it. Now listen to me. I am an American, and you don't like me. Make sure you tell people that. I am an imperialist son of a bitch, and you want me to leave your hotel as soon as possible."

"What are you going to do?"

"You don't want to know."

"I want to know."

I held her eye and decided she needed to know. "I am going to bring your daughter back. I am going to bring all the kids back. And I am going to kill every other son of a bitch at the mine and here in the village. But I can only do that if you play your part and play it well."

She stood and handed me her glass. Then she took my face in her hands and kissed me long and hard. When she was done, she left without a word.

After the door had closed, I washed and dried the glasses and the bottle. Then I took my cell and sent a message to the brigadier. It read, "Hey, Mom, I was thinking I'd pop over for lunch tomorrow."

I was surprised to receive a reply within thirty seconds: "I look forward to it."

SIX

I was up at six, spent an hour working out, and by seven-thirty, I was showered and dressed and on my way down for breakfast, planning to be on my way to Catamarca by eight. I entered the small breakfast room and sat at a table that had been set by an open window with tall green French shutters.

The door to the small kitchen opened a little more forcefully than was necessary, and Carla came in looking like she had just gotten out the wrong side of the bed and put her foot in the chamber pot. I was going to wish her a good morning, but she got there first and snapped, "This is Argentina, we don't do the full American breakfast. You can have toast, facturas, cream cheese, jelly or jam, coffee, tea or mate."

"I'll just have some toast and black coffee -"

"If you want eggs over easy, scrambled, sunny side up, bacon, waffles..."

"I don't want any of –"

She began to wave her hands around. "...you can get in your big RAM truck, go back to the airport, and fly right back to Texas, or wherever you comin' from!"

"Toast and coffee will be fine, thank you."

Across the road, I saw a woman peer out of her open front

door. I don't know if she spoke English, but Carla's tone was conveying everything she needed to know. She said, "Cream cheese *or* jam *or* jelly?"

"Just butter will be fine. Thank you."

She cocked a hip. "You paid for it, right? With your *American Express*. So I don't need your thanks. Thanks!"

I raised my voice. "Yeah, but I happen to have good manners, Carla. So if you'll just bring me my toast and coffee, that will be fine. *Thank you!*"

As she turned and stalked out, my cell started ringing. The screen told me it was Rosario, and I cursed softly under my breath before answering, "Good morning, you're up early."

"I didn't sleep much last night."

"I'm sorry to hear that. I hope that wasn't my fault."

"Only indirectly. I had a lot on my mind. Can we talk?"

"I have a meeting with my editor in Catamarca at noon -"

The door to the small kitchen burst open, and Carla appeared with a coffee pot and a basket of toast and pastries. She had what my gran used to describe as a face like a summons. She spoke over me as she approached the table.

"Jus' because you come here payin' with your *American Express*, it don't mean you gonna get special treatment." She dumped the coffee on the table and the basket beside it. "Here, in Argentina, everybody get treated the same. It don't matter if you are rich or poor."

I injected a sense of defeat into my voice and gestured at the cell by my ear. "Carla, I'm talking on the phone, can you please give it a rest?"

"You think because you are from the US you gonna have privileges? Because you are friend of the mayor—"

"Rosario's voice said, "What's going on?"

"Nothing. Carla is serving me humble pie for breakfast."

Carla leaned close to me, wagging her finger from side to side. "Pues no!" she said, breaking into Spanish. "Jus' because you are from US and have American Express don't make you special.

Here people work hard in the fields"—she pointed out the window, like there were fields out there instead of a street—"and we respect them for that, for their work, more than for their money!"

"Carla, I am talking on the telephone, do you mind?"

She stormed away and slammed the kitchen door, leaving me a breakfast fit for a king. Rosario said, "Is she being a problem? You need me to talk to her?"

"No, I guess the CIA hasn't left Uncle Sam much of a reputation south of the border. But I have a pretty thick skin, and I don't plan to stay here long. So it's not a problem. You want to come with me to Catamarca? We can talk on the way. If you don't mind killing time while I talk to my editor -"

There was an unexpectedly long silence. "What's your editor doing in Catamarca?"

"Passing through. It's all he ever does anywhere, pass through. We shouldn't be more than half an hour. Then you and I can have lunch."

There was a warm smile in her voice when she said, "That sounds like a plan, Harry."

"Shall I pick you up?"

"No, I'll come to you. How long do you need for your Argentine breakfast?"

I looked at the feast Carla had laid before me on the table. "Give me fifteen minutes and I'll meet you in reception."

I hung up and dug in. Carla passed and winked at me, then stopped and came back, frowning. "But everything I say is true, eh?"

I made an affirmative noise with my mouth full, and she went away sporting a smug smile on her face.

Half an hour later, I was in my RAM with Rosario beside me in Levis that did nothing to hide the exquisite shape of her legs and a purple silk blouse that did nice things for the rest of her.

We moved across the vast, flat plain at speed with the windows open and the warm, thin air battering our faces. It took her hair and spread it across her face, making her laugh as she pulled it away with her fingers and tied it in a loose bun behind her neck.

"Are you trying to shut me up?" she said, raising her voice over the wind.

I slowed as we approached the turn-off where I had seen the factory and killed the two men the night before. I glanced at her, smiling, looking for any expression on her face. There was nothing.

"I thought you wanted me to talk," she said more seriously.

"What is there, north and west," I asked, still smiling, "that gets men killed in the night?"

"You heard about that?"

"Carla doesn't exactly hold back. Add to that the fact that just about everything is the fault of the United States, and I am an American, and she becomes a scary mixture of syndicated news and the Conspiracy Channel."

She laughed like I'd been really witty, then went quiet.

"I remember her as a child. We used to play before I was sent to Buenos Aires. Her father had some land and owned the big house that is now the hotel. He was an enterprising man. But he was a socialist." She glanced at me. "An active socialist. Argentina suffered a big crisis at the turn of the millennium, you know. Most people in the West had no idea, but the country almost collapsed. Buenos Aires burned, the president fled in a helicopter!" She laughed.

"I remember."

She arched an eyebrow. "You were paying attention?"

"It was the casserole revolution. Everyone was in the streets banging kitchen utensils."

She nodded. "They set fire to the streets. People were killed. That was in the cities, but in the villages, things were bad too. Carla's father was a reformer. He wanted the village to become a cooperative to protect the families against poverty and give them a stronger voice. It was a nice idea but naïve."

"Yeah? What happened?"

"There were meetings in the municipality – the city hall – and Carlos, that was her father, he was very persuasive. The very poor, the people who were struggling, most of the people, supported his plans for reform."

I grunted. "It sounds like a familiar story. He threatened the interests of the one percent who were benefiting from the crisis."

"The mayor's father was Enrique McCormack. They were a Scottish family who settled here two hundred years ago and bought practically all the land around the village for practically nothing. As long as the other farmers were smallholders, they could not compete with him. But if they united as a cooperative, raising cattle for example, they could threaten his monopoly."

She went quiet. I glanced at her. She was staring out the open window at the miles of gnarled, twisted bushes that peppered the flat landscape.

"What happened?"

"He, his wife, and his son were butchered one night. The killers were never caught. Carla was the only survivor. She was just two years old. She was staying with her grandmother that weekend. When she came home, her family were all dead."

"You believe McCormack killed them?"

Her smile was humorless. "Don't you?"

We were approaching a fork in the road where a shrine had been built between the two branches. It was a surreal sight, decked with plastic flowers in a great, wire arch. It slipped by on our right, and the landscape began to change subtly. The gnarled bushes were replaced by small trees, and in the distance, you could see expanses of fields.

I said, "So he owns the land where the mine is." She didn't say anything. I looked at her. "The mine that's to the northwest, the lithium mine. Only it's not him now, is it? It's his son, Nelson."

She still didn't say anything. I pressed her.

"Is that who you had to talk to last night? To get permission to tell me about it?"

"Who are you?" She asked it with no particular inflection. I sighed like she was being slow.

"Come on, Rosario. Quit playing games. I'm a journalist. I write boring shit about how nice it is to go on vacation to remote places and absorb the real culture and eat the real cuisine. What I would like is to write stories the make front page news in the big papers and have documentaries made about my stories."

She was watching me carefully.

"Nobody knows better than you, Rosario, how important lithium is going to be in the next couple of decades. McCormack has animal cunning, but you? You're intelligent. You've got smarts. You know as well as I do that Argentina is set to become the Saudi Arabia of the electric age. So if there is a story at this mine, something really heavy, I can clean up. I can get a Pulitzer, make a million. And you can be a part of it."

"What do you think is going on there?" She laughed unexpectedly. "That is heavy, that can earn you a Pulitzer and a million dollars?"

I watched her a moment. The road was real straight as the gradient began to descend toward the lowlands.

"Something that could get two guys killed in the night?" I watched the road a moment, then added, "What gets two guys killed like that? While you and I were having dinner, there were two men out there, in the wilderness. What were they doing? More to the point, Rosario, what were they doing that upset somebody so much, they were shot dead?"

I caught the quick glance as she noted I'd gotten the cause of death wrong. She drew breath, thought better of it, and went quiet again. I said, "You called me this morning and asked if we could talk, but right now, it's hard to get one word out of you."

"You want to tone down the pressure, Harry? You're coming on real strong. This morning I wanted to talk. Right now, I am not so sure. Bring it down a notch or two."

I raised my shoulders an eighth of an inch. "I apologize. In my trade, that's how you get things done."

She was quiet for a moment looking out at the peaks that rose suddenly around us as we started to descend. I was surprised to see large concentrations of saguaro cactus on either side of the road. "I am not your trade," she said with a bitterness that made me look at her. "I am a person."

"I'm sorry."

"Nelson McCormack's father had a stroke ten years ago. He is confined to bed. He is in his mid eighties. He will die soon, but either way, Nelson has sole power of attorney. He effectively owns the land for many miles around the village of Poman, El Pajonal, the farms we have passed..." She trailed off and shrugged. "For many years, a century or more, this land had practically no value. But ten years ago, some people approached Nelson. There was lithium in his land, and lithium was the future. There was a lot of negotiating. I became involved for the first time five years ago. And a little over one year ago, they began constructing the mine and the processing plant."

I waited, but it seemed she wasn't going to say any more.

"Okay, but you want to tell me what the big secret is?"

We came to another intersection, and I turned left, away from the mountains, following the signs for Catamarca.

"A lot of people start up companies in remote places, Rosario. Some of those are mines, and some of them are even lithium mines. They are not all shrouded in mystery, and they don't all produce dead guys late at night in the -"

She cut across me suddenly. "What makes you so sure those dead men had anything to do with the mine?"

I smiled, then laughed. "Well, for one thing that it took you so long to come up with that question. But if that weren't enough, how about the fact that the only people out and about at that time of night in Poman last night – or any night - were employees of the mine? So who were they? Spies?"

She sighed and shook her head. "You are pushing too much."

I threw back my head and laughed a loud, unpleasant laugh. "Baby," I said, "I ain't even gotten started yet. So what were you going to tell me today, that the mayor did a deal to open a lithium mine? How is that news? Come on, Rosario. What's going down here? You know I'm going to find out anyway, and you can be sure you want to be with me and not against me."

She watched me for a moment with an arched eyebrow. "Are you threatening me?"

I gave her my most engaging lopsided smile. "Yeah, I guess I am."

She laughed. "You son of a bitch."

"You got that right. But I can also be a damn good friend."

We were approaching the suburbs of Catamarca, and suddenly everything was lush and green, like a different world from the one we had left up in the mountains. I told her, "I'm going to drop you in the Plaza 25 de Mayo. That gives you an hour to think things over. Then we have lunch, and by then I will need to know where we stand."

Once again, she didn't answer.

I dropped her at the Mostaza, a hamburger joint on the square, then took a circuitous route to the brigadier's hotel and parked in the hotel parking lot. From there, I took the elevator to the top floor and exited to a corridor carpeted in burgundy with small art deco lamps on the walls. I turned right and went to the door at the end. There I took out my cell and sent an encoded, prearranged message. A couple of seconds later, a guy the size and consistency of a small train opened the door and grinned at me.

"Hey, Harry," he said in a voice like he was grinding bricks with his esophagus. "The bwigadier's on the balcony. You want some cawfee, or you gonna have a man's dwink?"

SEVEN

I TOLD CHUCK I'D HAVE A MAN'S DWINK, AND WHILE HE went to get it, I made my way out to the balcony, where I found the brigadier in a cream linen suit reading the *New York Times* from behind a pair of black Wayfarers. He had a glass of Irish whiskey straight up sitting on the table beside him.

"Sit down, Harry." He said it without looking up from the paper. "Has Chuck offered you a drink?"

"No." I pulled out a chair and sat. "He offered me a man's dwink. It's a little early, but what the hell."

"Quite so." He folded the paper and dropped it beside his glass. "Report. Where do we stand?"

Chuck came out with a generous Bushmills and a bowl of peanuts. He patted my shoulder with what felt like approval and went back inside. I sipped.

"The mine is there, and it looks pretty big. Hard to see precisely because it is very flat and the only vegetation consists of small, gnarled bushes. So if I approach by day, they are going to see me long before I get a good look at them."

"You went last night?"

"I had a look. I got within half a mile and saw the processing plant. It was in full swing, and it is processing a lot of crude material. The mayor of the village of Poman, Nelson McCormack, owns practically all the land around there. His grandfather bought it cheap back in the day. Dad's out for the count with a stroke, so Nelson runs the show via a power of attorney."

I picked up a couple of peanuts, chewed, and organized my thoughts.

"Nelson McCormack has an assistant, Rosario Fuentes. She's interesting."

"In what way, precisely?" There was no mistaking the dry irony in his voice.

"In every way you can imagine. But most of all because she is highly educated, her English is flawless, and she is clearly the product of an expensive, international education. But she claims to be the daughter of the village doctor, who invested every penny he had in getting her a good education in Buenos Aires. She has a law degree and claims to work for an important law firm which she hasn't named. Yet she is there in Poman, assisting the mayor in negotiations with the mining corporation. She puts it down to Latin American culture and loyalty."

He grunted.

"My view is that she is employed by the mine, the mayor has a stake in the mine, and she has been planted on me to find out if I am who I say I am and to steer me away from investigating too deeply. So far what they have done is urge me to explore south and east and steer clear of north and west."

"That is very suggestive, but not quite compelling."

"I'm getting there. Last night, while I was having a look at the processing plant, I was detected, and two guys came up in a Jeep. I figured it was imperative nobody knew I was watching them, and also they were armed and didn't look like they wanted to chat. So I killed them."

"Knife?"

"Yes. I went back to my hotel and told the receptionist I had been in my room all afternoon and evening -"

"The receptionist..."

I filled him in about Carla, then added, "And I called Rosario and invited her out to dinner. I made like I had a sideline in investigative journalism and I was interested in what was going on north and west of the village, and why they were so secretive.

"That night Carla came to my room. The bodies had been found, and she put two and two together and made me as the killer. That was when she told me all the kids in the village had been taken to a special school at the mine, including her daughter."

"Ah."

"This morning, Rosario phoned as I was leaving. She had something to tell me. I brought her with me. She's at the Mostaza on the plaza down the road. I spent the trip here trying to pump her about who killed the two guys last night."

"Good."

"When we're done here, I am going to take her to lunch, and she is going to tell me something. I don't know what. Probably bullshit, but I figure we are ninety percent sure what's going down at the mine. We need to be getting ordnance in place and making a plan of attack."

"I agree. What do you need?"

"Why haven't we got better satellite imagery of the site?"

"Frankly, I don't know. Some of our people are speculating that there might simply be high concentrations of dust in the air, others are suggesting moisture or gas refracting light, which is very unlikely at that altitude. But it's clear they are doing something which is distorting the satellite imagery as it passes over that area."

"So I am going in partially blind."

"Yes. We could send in a drone at low altitude, but that would only serve to alert them."

"I need to know where the school is so I can make it safe and get the kids out. I don't even know how many kids there are there."

He sighed and took a long pull on his whiskey. "It's worse than that, Harry. My sources tell me there are about a dozen villages and settlements in the province of Catamarca that are entirely Indian, are unregistered and the inhabitants are not in any census."

"This is not a job for one man alone, sir. This is a job for a patrol, or two. One for the assault and the other to get the kids out."

"I know. And I agree. Unfortunately, that's not an option."

I'd known the brigadier long enough to know that if he said something was not an option, it wasn't an option. And something that was branded into you in the regiment was that you don't waste time regretting and wishing things were otherwise. You work with what you've got, and you make what you've got work.

"So," I said, "I'll need to take out their generator and their backup generator. We have to assume they have one of each, and I will have to guess where they're located."

He took a handful of peanuts and started putting them in his mouth one at a time.

"Then we are talking C4 or mines. Rockets would be too risky. You identify the generator by finding the building with all the cables coming out of it. If the cables have been laid underground, then the generator building will be the one with no obvious use and plenty of ventilation."

I nodded. "Okay. The processing plant is brightly lit at night, it covers about a hundred and fifty acres. The mine itself it was impossible to gauge. I'd say thousands of acres."

"So we have a catch 22. You need to cut the power in order to get in to the processing plant, but you need to get into the processing plant to cut the power."

"And we can't use airpower or rockets."

We sat staring at each other for a long moment. Only somebody who knew us really well would have detected the smile. He looked past me and called, "Chuck, bring a notepad and a pen." Chuck emerged carrying a notepad that looked like a postage stamp in his hand. He sat and pulled a pen from an inside pocket.

The brigadier said, "Make a note. C4." He glanced at me. "How many pounds...?"

———

SHE WAS STILL SITTING at the Mostaza. She had a glass of sparkling water in front of her with lemon and ice, and she was reading a magazine called *Caras* that seemed to be all glossy photographs of weird, skinny people with enough text to convey the fact that they had gotten married, gotten divorced, had an affair, or were suspected of being about to do one of those three things.

She looked up as I sat and threw the magazine on the table. 'When you read this shit," she said with a sudden look of disgust, "you realize the average IQ really is just one hundred."

"Did something happen to make you mad, or did you deliberately choose a magazine you knew would make you mad?"

She gave a small sigh and observed the people passing by for a moment. "You happened to make me mad."

I smiled. "Let's put a positive reframe on it. At least I didn't go unnoticed."

"What does your editor say?"

"Explore to the south and east. If Poman has nothing to offer, move south to the ski resorts—Patagonia, Tierra del Fuego."

"It's good advice."

"Keep on like this and I'm going to feel rejected and unloved."

She tilted her head on one side, and her expression became hard. "Do you understand, Harry, that you are causing me a lot of problems?"

"Yes." I leaned forward. "Now I have a couple of questions for you. Do you understand that I can cause you a lot more problems? And do you understand that I don't care? Now I am going to tell you what we are going to do. We are going to go to a restaurant of my choosing, we are going to have a nice luncheon, and you are going to tell me what gives with the north and the west.

And just in case you still don't fully understand, this is not negotiable."

She frowned. "I tell you to go to hell and call for a car. What are you going to do?"

I laughed. "Let me tell you where I'd start. I'd start by calling my friend at the *Washington Post* to let him know two men were murdered by security guards outside a remote facility in the Andes north of Catamarca. The facility is claimed to be a mine, but experts say it is using some kind of cloaking device that blurs satellite imagery, and local villagers -"

"Stop."

"How about some lunch?" I stood and offered her my arm. She stared at it like she wanted to cut it off and feed it to a dog. I said, "Play along."

She took my arm, and we walked for ten minutes down a cute, pedestrianized street with plenty of shady trees and stone benches called Pavadavia. It had triumphed in managing to look like a pedestrianized street anywhere in the Western world.

"So this morning you phoned me and you were sweet and friendly and you wanted to talk. After I talk with my editor, now you are hostile and want me to go away. Feel like explaining?"

"Twenty years ago, Argentina was on the edge of bankruptcy."

"That's not news."

"Shut up and listen to me.

Twenty years before that we went into a stupid war with the UK over two islands nobody wants and that never belonged to us anyway! We were a crippled economy and practically a third world country." I waited. After a moment, she went on. "Slowly, very painfully, we have started to climb out of this hole, and now all the emigrants who went to Spain and Europe to escape the poverty and corruption here are coming back. Because the quality of life and the standard of living here is better than in Europe."

"Is this going somewhere?"

We had come to a restaurant on the corner called Antaño. It was painted an ugly, military green, but there were good aromas wafting out. I opened the door, and she went in ahead of me. The ceiling was high, and there were a lot of old things hanging on the walls, everything from rusty keys to bits of plows and photographs of old things. The tables and chairs were heavy, solid wood, and there was an agreeable authentic rustic feel to the place. We sat, and I ordered a couple of cold beers and a couple of menus.

I drew breath, but she cut me short. "Yes, it is going somewhere. Are you in a hurry? You need to be somewhere? No? So give your mouth a rest and use your ears for a bit."

"Wow."

"Yeah, wow. So today, Argentina is a prosperous country with political stability and a good quality of life. But it is not a rich, powerful country. Now you listen to me, Harry." She leaned forward and wagged a finger at me. "You go a bit to the north and you come to Venezuela. Venezuela is one of the biggest oil producers in the world. Now I am asking you, did Venezuela benefit from its oil?"

I gave my head a small shake. "Nope."

"And when Venezuela elected a president who wanted to change things so that the people of Venezuela could benefit, what happened?"

"He wasn't smart about it."

"What happened?"

"You know what happened. The CIA moved in and triggered a coup."

"There is a club, and you know this. The countries that control the energy sources of the planet. The United States, Saudi, UK, Russia, and China." She held up her hand with her fingers splayed. "Five. There are other countries, but those are the five who control the energy sources of this world."

"Okay, so what's your point?"

"My point is that over the next twenty to fifty years, one of two things is going to happen. One, Argentina will replace Saudi Arabia as the main source for energy..."

"As the biggest lithium producer."

"Yes. Or two, the United States will take possession of Argentina, cripple her politically, and reduce her to a dependent wreck so that they can take control of the lithium."

I grunted and sat back to allow the waiter to deliver the beers and the menus. I had expected a whole range of answers, but I had not expected this. It almost had the ring of truth to it.

"So you're telling me there is a lithium mine out there -"

"That is a matter of public record. You know that."

I kept on going. "But you are keeping a low profile so that competing interests don't move in and take over."

She gave a small shrug and picked up her beer. "More or less." She sipped. "After our conversation last night, I thought maybe I could trust you to collaborate with us. But after your behavior today, I no longer think so. That is the reason for my change in attitude."

"And the two guys who were shot last night. What were they, CIA spies?"

"I don't know who they were. How do you know they were shot?"

I mixed a frown with a smile and made irony. "I don't know they were shot. I assume they were shot. I assume the security guards at your mine carry guns."

She gave a couple of small nods. "It's not my mine, Harry. So what are you going to do now? Are you going to betray us and have Argentina dragged back into chaos again? Now that art and culture and intellectual discourse are flowering here and we can look to a bright future."

I sighed loudly. "Either you're telling the truth, or you are really smart. What'll you have?"

"Steak."

"Sounds good to me. How do you have it?"

"Singed, with lots of blood." I looked up at her. She met my gaze and gave her head a small shake. "What? That's how I like my steak."

EIGHT

We shared a plate of Andes Sebago salmon with sautéed asparagus tips and fennel root, with a glass of Catena Alta Chardonnay that tasted like a bowl of ripe pears and peaches. We ate in strained silence until the plate was clean, then she leaned back in her chair and sighed as she dabbed her mouth with her napkin.

"I owe you an apology, Harry."

"You do?"

"Trust is a big issue for me, and you must admit you come on pretty strong."

I was going to ask her what possible reason she could have for trusting me but decided instead to sip my wine and frown like I cared that trust was a big issue for her. She gave a small laugh.

"You may have picked that up from what I was telling you about Argentina and our struggle for self-sufficiency and independence. The West has not been a good friend to us, but -" She faltered and looked down at her glass in her fingers. "On a personal level, I have been betrayed too often. Some people who believe they know what is best for you – my father, my mother, my whole family—" She stared right into my eyes. "You think if I had been given the choice, I would not have picked family and love over education? And in school the teacher who bullied and abused the children knowing their families would not protect them." She looked out of the window at the bright day outside. "And the lovers, men who care nothing for your mind or your soul, but only for your body and the efficiency of your work."

"What reason have I given you to believe I am any different? You were the one who used the word blackmail. Correct me if I am wrong, but I seem to remember putting you in a corner to try and force a story out of you that you did not want to give me." I gave my head a little shake. "Now you're apologizing for not trusting me?"

She gave a little laugh, paused and gave a bigger one, then looked at me with strangely fond eyes.

"Harry, you are tough. I can see that. I would not like to be on the wrong side of you. But I can also read in your eyes that you are a good man. Okay, so you tried to force this story out of me. What for? Because you believe there is an injustice being perpetrated at the lithium mine, and if there is, you want to expose it."

She sat and smiled, slowly spinning the wine in her glass. Suddenly I felt uncomfortable, like I'd woken up in the street with no clothes on.

"I am very observant," she went on. "I have seen how you speak to me, how you speak to Mr. McCormack, the waiters. I can see you are a dangerous man, but I can see also something else."

"What do you think you can see, Rosario?"

"Respect."

I laughed out loud. "Bullshit!"

The smile didn't fade from her face; she just raised an eyebrow to let me know she could see right through the front.

"Your default approach to every person, Mr. Harry Bauer, is respect." She pointed at me. "If somebody betrays that respect or comes against you, the Lord have mercy on their souls. But your opening position, pending further data, is respect."

"I wouldn't let that idea run away with you."

She ignored me. "Let me tell you, Harry, it is a position that I like and that attracts me. I have seen it in very few men besides my father. You became very aggressive in the car, on the way down here, and that made me doubt. But when I thought about it, I understood. So I apologize for not trusting you."

The steaks arrived with a bottle of Adrianna Vineyard malbec. He poured some for me to try. She watched me. I gave him the nod. He poured and left. When he'd gone, she said, "I am going to arrange for you to come and visit the mine."

"When?"

"You're welcome. It depends on what time we get back. Maybe this evening if it's not too late. Otherwise maybe tomorrow. It depends on who is around and who is in charge."

I cut into the steak. It was tender the way only Argentine beef is. "I don't want a sanitized guided tour, Rosario. I appreciate what you're doing, but I need to see it as it is."

"I know," she said and sipped her very red wine from the big glass. "You will."

She watched me eat, and I watched her back with a full mouth. "How much of a bastard are you?" she asked after a while.

"Make up your mind. You just told me I was respectful and noble."

"Until crossed. Have you ever killed anyone?"

I sighed at my plate as I mopped up blood and oil with a hunk of warm, crusty bread.

"I try to avoid killing people unless they ask me stupid questions. I told you I was in special forces in Iraq and Afghanistan. We weren't there developing a meaningful dialogue with those guys."

"I'm trying to work out what lines you've crossed."

"What for?"

"To know who I'm dealing with."

I drained my glass and set it down carefully on the table. "I have crossed them all, Rosario. There is nothing left for me to cross. I try to be a good guy, but whatever needs doing, I'll do it, and I won't hesitate. So I have two questions for you: What is it you want me to do? And how much does it pay?"

Her eyes were alive, but it was hard to tell what with. She giggled, then gave a small laugh. "Down, boy. I was only asking." Then, "Boy! This wine is going to my head!"

On the way back to collect the car, as we strolled down the pedestrianized Pavadavia, she took my arm, willingly this time and with both of hers, leaning slightly against me.

Just outside Catamarca, she closed her eyes. Whether she was sleeping or avoiding further conversation was hard to tell. She didn't snore, which I told myself with some irony was good news.

We traversed the green, fertile valley at a leisurely pace, and after half an hour, we passed the village of Chumbicha and shortly after that came to the intersection. There I turned north and started moving toward the mountains in the distance. Here we entered woodland, and though the trees were small, in the afternoon light, they seemed to close in, and I was aware that we were the only car on the long, solitary road. We followed that road for some eight miles among the dense undergrowth before the road started to wind and climb into the foothills. And that was where I first glimpsed the car closing in behind us. I registered that I was not driving slowly, so he must be shifting at a good pace.

I began to slow as I took the corners, thinking I'd rather have a boy racer pulling away ahead of me than getting up my ass behind me.

A couple of short straights and a couple of tight bends and he was twenty or thirty feet behind me. We weren't in an area where it was smart to pass, but I remembered there was an area up ahead where I could pull over and let him go on his way. He closed in, so he was maybe fifteen feet away. The thought crossed my mind that I could put my hazards on, stop, go back, and break his arms. But then I remembered that, according to Rosario, I was respect-ful. I also noticed in my mirror that there were two of them, both guys in their thirties, and they weren't laughing.

I came around the next bend and saw the area of dirt beside the road where I could pull off. I also saw a car pulled across the road and a guy in plain clothes holding up his hand for me to stop, indicating with the other I should pull over onto the dirt. I glanced in the mirror. The guy behind me had his hazards on. He was in the middle of the road, and the passenger was climbing out.

As I pulled over, I shook Rosario. "Are these friends of yours?"

She was blinking and frowning. "What?" She took in the scene and added, "What the hell?"

I stopped. Two guys, one from each car, were walking over toward us at a pace that meant business. I noticed they both had semi-automatics on their hips. In the meantime, the cars were taking up positions a few feet away that would make it really difficult to drive away faster than they could shoot you. I was still wondering if they were cops, but I was pretty sure they weren't. I opened the window.

"Buenas tardes," I said in my worst Spanish.

They had their weapons in their hands now. One of them, a tall, bony guy with too much hair, had gone to the passenger side and was wrenching open Rosario's door. The other guy, who had aviators and a pencil moustache, was pointing his weapon at me and shouting, "Baje del vehiculo!"

I could hear Rosario screaming somewhere between terror and rage. I nodded, opened the door, and swung down. I put my hands up and said, "Que pasa?" The two drivers were there by now. One of them looked Indian and had a very black ponytail. He was frisking me while the other guy, who had red hair and freckles, was taking his time frisking Rosario. The grin on his face said he was enjoying it.

The pencil moustache snapped, "Allí! Allí!" and jabbed his Glock toward where Rosario was standing beside the road. Behind her was dense foliage and undergrowth. I figured that was where they wanted the bodies to fall. I shrugged, squinted, and shook my head, like I was stupid and didn't understand. I added, "No comprende" for good measure. He did what he was supposed to do. He snarled, "Allí!" and jabbed his weapon at the side of the road again.

For two-thirds of a second his weapon was trained on a tree. I had a whole half-second to spare, because I only needed a quarter.

I leaned a quarter inch to my left as my left hand closed on the barrel and the blade of my right hand smashed into his wrist joint. By the time my right hand had slipped over the butt and pulled the trigger, we hadn't made the quarter second.

His head whiplashed, and what brains he had erupted from the back of his head and became part of the Argentine highway system. By that time I had turned and put a round through the abundant hair of the tall guy. He knelt slowly before Rosario, and, though he was dead, he looked confused.

The redhead was fumbling for his gun while his brain tried to adjust and make sense of what had just happened. He never made it. It was a fractional adjustment from where my hand had been to shoot his pal. I squeezed, and the slug punched through his right eye and out the back of his head. His brain became fertilizer, which is an appropriate use for bull and horse manure, I guess.

I knew the Indian with the ponytail had had enough time to react. So I spun and rammed the butt of the Glock into his face. The timing was tight, because as I was doing that, he was ramming his fist in a right hook into my belly. His position was bad, and I had knocked him off balance, but he was strong, and it hurt.

As he staggered, I ignored the pain, stepped forward, and delivered a right straight to his jaw. When that connects, it's curtains. You go unconscious. His eyes rolled, and as his knees sagged, I stepped behind him and put my arm around his neck with the crook of my elbow under his chin. I gripped my left bicep and put my left forearm across the back of his neck. Then I squeezed. The weight of his body did the rest.

I let him drop. Rosario was gaping, staring at me. I said, "Don't waste time. Get in the car. We need to get out of here."

I pulled open the driver's door.. She was still staring at me. I snapped, "*Now!*"

She clambered in. I eased between the parked cars, and we sped away.

She didn't talk until we were approaching the high plain. Then she shook her head and said, "That, what you did. How? They were nothing to you. You just..."

"It's not a virtue or a defect, Rosario. It's just training. Don't think about it."

After a moment, she closed her eyes again and seemed to go to sleep. By the time we'd crossed the plain and were approaching the village, the sun was moving into late afternoon, and the light was turning bronze. I reached out and gave her arm a gentle shake.

"Where do you want me to leave you?"

She opened her eyes and blinked. "At the entrance to the village. On the right. There is a Spanish ranch set back from the road."

"That's yours?"

"My father's." She gave a small shrug. "Yes, mine."

Two minutes later, I pulled up outside the ranch. "You'll call me about seeing the mine?"

She opened the door, then surprised me by leaning across and kissing me on the corner of my mouth.

"Thank you. You saved my life. I'll call you in an hour or two, before dinner."

She swung down, slammed the door, and walked to the big, wrought iron gates. There she pushed them open and disappeared inside.

I rolled slowly back to the hotel. I checked my room for bugs and called the brigadier.

"Some development?"

"Yeah, you could say so. Suddenly I am the blue-eyed boy. She can tell I am respectful of others and have good intentions. In the same breath, she wants to know what lines I have crossed as a special operative and how much of a bad boy I really am."

He grunted, then sighed. "What can I tell you you don't already know? Maybe she's grooming you, maybe she's setting you up, and maybe she is sincere but turned on by dangerous men. With women, it is very hard to tell."

I echoed his sigh. "Makes you wonder."

"Wonder?"

"What could Adam have gotten if he'd thrown in another rib, a kidney and his left pinky."

He laughed. "I have made the arrangements. I'll let you know when we are good to go. Meantime, play along and see if she tries to lead you anywhere. Keep me posted."

"Right. There's one other thing. We were ambushed on the way back. Four guys in two cars."

"You took care of them?"

"Yeah."

"How did they treat her?"

I thought about it, staring out of the French windows at the street below. "If I was a billionaire bad guy, I'd want to kill the guy who frisked her. He enjoyed himself. But she wasn't hurt, except in her vanity."

"Doesn't tell us much. Keep me posted."

I hung up and lay on the bed to think. She'd call soon to make an appointment to see the mine, maybe tonight. What then?

NINE

As it was, the call came as I was climbing out of the shower at just after eight-thirty. I answered it wet, wiping water from my eyes.

"Yeah?"

"How are you feeling?"

"Good. Did you get over the shock? You should lie down and have a whiskey."

"That's what I did. I also spoke to Nelson and a couple of other people. They want to talk to you."

"Tonight?"

"No. Two of them are flying in from the States. They'll be here tomorrow."

"That soon?" I laughed. "Haven't they got lives?"

"Don't flatter yourself, Harry. They were coming anyway."

I nodded. "Right. Is this the same United States you were so worried was going to take over the show?"

"Actually, no. It's a different United States altogether. Stop grilling me, Harry. We'll have dinner tomorrow night, and I think they might have a proposal for you."

"What about tonight?"

The question surprised me as much as it must have surprised

her. It was genuine, and I meant it. She was quiet so long I thought maybe she wasn't going to answer. Then she said, "I could come over and we could give each other a massage before dinner. But that probably wouldn't be a good idea."

"We'll have to agree to disagree on that one."

"I'll call you tomorrow, Harry."

And she hung up.

I finished toweling myself and got dressed turning over the phrase 'No, it's a different United States altogether.' Whichever way I turned it, it either made no sense or the sense was totally contradictory.

Unless it was a lie, and then, after just a little thought, it made perfect sense.

I went and dined alone, returned to the hotel by eleven, and was up and dressed by six a.m. to have my enormous Argentine breakfast in the small breakfast room.

At six-thirty, I took my truck and wasted the day exploring south and east of Poman, among the cattle ranches, the hunting lodges, and the vineyards. Rosario and Nelson were not wrong; they were places that would definitely attract tourism if *Vagabond* magazine ever sent a reporter here. So I made notes, mainly mental ones, and pretended to myself that I was that reporter so that I could talk about it all when we had dinner that night.

If we had dinner. If they didn't just throw me in a mine and shoot me.

I got back to the hotel at five p.m. Carla wasn't around, and I went up to my room to shower and change. At six, as I was pulling on my boots and strapping the Fairbairn and Sykes to my ankle, I heard a chopper fly low over the town.

A different United States altogether.

I called the brigadier.

"Harry."

"In the next half hour or so, they are going to come and get me."

"Who are, Harry?"

"Rosario and a couple or three guys who just flew in from the States. They arrived by helicopter a while ago, and their intention is to have dinner and show me the mine. I can't say no, but there's not a lot I can do to protect myself, either."

"If necessary, you must abort, you know that."

"Yeah, I know. But every day I spend contemplating my navel is another day those kids are being used as slaves. We don't know what conditions they are being kept in or how they are being treated."

"I agree, but you are not much use to them dead, are you, Harry?"

"Not much. Have you got a backup if I get killed?"

"Yes, of course, but we'd be starting from zero, and it could take weeks. Our operatives don't get killed, Harry. It's the other way around."

I sighed. "Have the materials been delivered?"

"They are out for delivery now. Should be complete by midnight."

"Okay, I'll give it some thought and reserve a decision till I hear from Rosario."

"You understand we can't depend on Argentine law enforcement in this business, don't you?"

"Yeah, I kind of got that."

"Keep me posted, and abort at any time you feel you should. Don't wait too long."

I hung up telling myself I had a hunch that ship had already sailed. It wasn't long after that the phone on my bedside table rang. It had obviously been fixed. When I answered, a man's voice spoke. It was gravelly and East Coast educated, the way Boston billionaires sound when they hunt and ride horses a lot. The voice said, "Mr. Bauer?"

"Yes."

"I am a guest of Rosario Fuentes. We are having a small, informal gathering for dinner at her house, and I wondered if you would like to join us. I understand you have some questions regarding our operations in Catamarca."

I didn't think. I said, "Sure. That sounds great. I was just talking to my editor and my attorney. What time do you want me?"

There was no mistaking the steel in his voice when he said, "Right now. I'm downstairs."

"Oh," I let my voice smile nicely. "Well, that's perfect timing then, isn't it?"

I thought about packing the Sig but in the end decided against it on the grounds that it might cause more problems than it solved. If I had to shoot somebody, I was pretty sure there would be enough guns around for me to borrow one. The thought made me smile as I stepped out onto the gallery landing and made my way down the stairs.

He had on a cream linen suit that probably cost more than the Mercedes that was parked outside. His hair was silver and made immobile by some kind of fixative spray, and the perfect white teeth made him look like an exquisitely manicured wolf.

I knew him. As he held out his hand, I recognized him. He kept a low profile and he stayed out of the news, but I had been in DC often enough with the brigadier to have had him pointed out to me. I took his hand, and he said, "Kit O'Hanlon. I understand you write for *Vagabond* -"

"No."

His eyebrows said he was surprised. "No? But Rosario -"

"I am a freelance journalist, Mr. O'Hanlon. I like to travel, so I sometimes publish in *Vagabond*, sometimes in *Survival* and *Weapons Magazine* and many others." I smiled. "I have even been known to write fiction sometimes."

"Fascinating. Well, you can tell us all about it over dinner. Rosario has told us all about you, and we are eager to know more."

We climbed into the car. He didn't buckle up but made a tight U-turn and headed out toward the ranch where I had left

Rosario earlier. He glanced at me, laughed, and gestured at the dash. "I removed the fuse so it would stop telling me to put on my seatbelt. I haven't much time for AI or machines that tell me what to do. In fact, I haven't much time for rules in general. Man is never greater than when he breaks the rules."

"Sounds like Nietzsche while taking acid with Maleclypse the Younger."

He laughed too loud and pounded the steering wheel with his fist. "I love it!" he said. "I love it! Actually I was paraphrasing General Patton, but Mark Twain and Arnold Schwarzenegger have said similar things."

I observed his profile a moment and said quietly, "It's a lesson anyone who's gotten past first base has had to learn."

He flashed a look at me with narrowed eyes. "Right?"

He was quiet for a bit. As we turned off the blacktop onto Rosario's dirt drive, he said, "The rules were made for the sheep. If you are a farmer or a hunter, what the hell do you need the rules for?"

I saw the big iron gate give a little jump and start to swing gently open. I said quietly, "To avoid getting shot by other farmers or hunters."

He gave a grin that expressed more hunger than amusement. "Yeah, there is that," he agreed.

The house was bigger than it looked from the road. It was a large, rambling Spanish building with corrugated terracotta roofs and several internal patios. Kit led me through the big double front doors which stood spilling light onto the terracotta paved terrace and into a large, very spacious living room with a vast open fireplace and plate glass doors that stood open onto an internal patio with a well and a superabundance of potted flowers, palms, and fruit trees. I made a mental note that if I ever decided to change my career, I should become an Andean doctor in a tiny village. This guy made enough to keep this house and send his daughter to Buenos Aires for a private education.

Rosario saw us and approached with both hands held out and a very special kind of smile on her face. "Kit," she said, and then more softly, "Harry."

She took my hand in both of hers and made the kiss on my cheek linger half a second longer than she needed to. "Come and meet the gang."

The gang, aside from Kit O'Hanlon, was two men and a woman. She took my hand and led me toward the cold fireplace, where the gang stood watching me. With the hand that wasn't holding mine, she gestured toward a short man of five foot two or three. He was wearing a burgundy brocade waistcoat, a yellow bowtie, and an expression of ill-concealed contempt.

"This is Nigel Hunt. Without his generosity, this project would never have got off the ground."

He didn't hold out his hand, so I nodded at him and said, "How do you do" like I really didn't give a damn how he did. Rosario was gesturing to the other guy, who was in his late twenties or very early thirties and was wearing a Snoopy sweatshirt and hair so short you could see his scalp. Rosario was saying, "This is Mat Coren, who has a genius for convincing people they have an imperative need to buy things that don't really exist."

Mat rolled his eyes with no sign of humor and held out a hand like a dead trout for me to shake.

"I sell algorithms," he said like he was exhausted explaining that to people. "Without algorithms"—he turned to Rosario—"as I have told you hundreds of times, we would still be living in the trees – that's if we survived at all."

"I know, darling, and this is Lady Angela Liu. The genius who makes everything happen."

Lady Angela Liu was six foot tall and slim without being skinny with very long arms and legs that seemed to be endowed with a life of their own. She also had a curious combination of Caucasian and Chinese features that made her as beautiful as she was unusual. Her face did something that in anybody else would have been a smile, and her hand rose toward my lips apparently of its own accord. I took it, felt compelled to kiss it, and told her, "It's a pleasure, Lady Angela."

Kit joined us and handed me a generous glass of whiskey, muttered something about appreciating a good Irish whiskey, and Lady Angela turned and moved toward the indoor patio, like something out of Tim Burton's *Mars Attacks*.

We followed.

There was an octagonal, white marble fountain splashing among abundant flowers in brilliantly decorated flowerpots. Beside it, there was a white wrought iron table, a bamboo recliner, a dark wood rocking chair with a couple of cushions that had seen better days, four bamboo chairs shaped like couches, and a bamboo throne that would have done justice to Emmanuelle. The arrangement managed to be both artificial and homey at the same time.

Lady Angela took the recliner, Rosario took the rocking chair, Nigel the Brocade Waistcoat took the Emmanuelle, and the rest of us took the bamboo sofas. Rosario started saying, "I hope you like roast lamb, Harry. Mateo has slaughtered two lambs for dinner -"

"We are all insane." It was Lady Angela. They all turned to look at her. I looked at them in turn. They weren't rolling their eyes with that *Angie's off again!* look. They were interested in what she was going to say.

"The secret to immense wealth, Harry, is understanding other people's insanity."

I knew I had to answer, but I also knew that telling her that was bullshit would not help my cause. So I said, "Alistair Crowley once told a young British aristocrat that he would sell him the secret of unlimited temporal power for ten thousand pounds sterling. The young fellow wrote him a check right there on the spot and handed it over. Crowley gave him a slip of paper on which he had written, 'There is one born every minute.'"

She smiled. "That was my great grandfather. He learned the lesson well."

"Alistair Crowley was your great grandfather or the young noble?" As she drew breath to answer, I interrupted her. "I heard George Bush was descended from Alistair Crowley through his mother. But I think that's just a myth."

I had interrupted the great lady, and the four faces that were staring at me were telling me that was not cool. My smile as I sipped my whiskey told them I disagreed. I turned my gaze on Kit.

"So what's the story at the mine? I heard your guards killed two men the other night." Three eyebrows arched at me, and Rosario looked at her lap.

Kit said, "Who told you that?"

I shook my head and pushed out my lower lip. "You know, I don't remember. Village gossip. Or it may have been Ruth and Graham, who were passing through on the bicycles. Why, is it not true?"

Lady Angela turned her head on her long neck and looked at Rosario. "Darling, did you not explain to Harry about what happened?"

A sudden alertness to a dynamic I had not been aware of till then made me say, "Sure she did. I'm just curious to see if you give me the same explanation." I laughed out loud. "I'm an investigative, freelance reporter, right? That's why you invited me here tonight. And it's why I came. I'm happy to drink this great whiskey and make small talk all night long and then draw my own conclusions. But I think it would be most beneficial to all of us if we cut the bullshit and talked to each other. What do you say?" I smiled at Rosario and added, "And for the record, Rosario has been nothing but professional and extremely patient with a guy who can be a real pain in the ass when he wants to be."

It was Nigel the Burgundy Waistcoat who answered.

"Thank you for cutting through the bullshit, Mr. Bauer. Now we know where we stand. So let me ask you a question. On the way back from your visit to your, um, *editor*, this morning"—he paused to allow the heavy irony to sink in—"four men attempted to assassinate you and Rosario. We have heard in detail how you dispatched them in something under five seconds. Would you like to explain to us how someone with those skills winds up writing travel journalism?"

TEN

THE ATMOSPHERE WAS WHAT YOU COULD HAVE CALLED heavily charged. They were all staring at me except Rosario, who was staring at her feet. When you have been stared at by a dozen Taliban holding AK47s, four billionaires holding cocktails doesn't really get your pulse going. I gave a small shrug.

"It's not as unlikely as you might think. When you get that stuff drummed into you on a daily basis over almost a decade, it becomes automatic."

"That is not my point, Mr. Bauer. My point is, a man of your age with your expertise could be commanding a six-figure salary. So what are you doing here, writing about the dubious delights of Poman?"

"Sure, Mr. Hunt, I could command a six-figure salary, but I am done taking salaries. Because behind every salary there is some guy giving you orders. And I am also done taking orders. So I freelance. Maybe Poman will net me just a few thousand bucks, maybe it will net me a Pulitzer and a *New York Times* bestseller. But the guy who gets to decide that is me." I leaned forward with my elbows on my knees and pointed at Mat the Nerd. "Let me ask you something, Mat. You're a billionaire. But what is more important to you, the billions of dollars you own or the power they give you?"

He didn't answer; he just blinked. I leaned back, nodded, and turned to Lady Angela. "That's what I thought. So, Lady Angela, I killed four men this morning in less than five seconds because I was trained by the best special ops regiment on the planet, bar none. So if you guys are done with your questions, I have a couple of questions for you." I was still holding her eye and thinking she looked oddly reptilian. "The first is this: Why did you send four men to kill me today? The second is, having done that and seen how I dealt with them"—I pointed around the large, spacious room—"how come you've got no security here? I didn't bring a gun, but do you realize how long it would take me to dispatch the four of you?" I gave my head a small shake. "Less than four seconds." I pointed at Nigel, who was frozen rigid. "Less time than it would take you to sip your drink and put your glass down."

There was a protracted silence, broken eventually by Rosario. She gave a small, unhappy laugh. "I invite you to dinner and you threaten to kill my other guests?"

I didn't look at her. I kept my eyes on Nigel. "I don't respond well to being interrogated. And I respond even worse to veiled threats and insinuations that I am working as an industrial spy. How about we start again from the top and you cut out the Mr. Bauer crap, *Nigel?*"

I figured I had the meeting on my terms and shifted my attention to Lady Angela Liu. "Let's start with whether your mine ordered a hit on me this morning. Did it?"

She closed her eyes. "Of course not."

"Why of course?"

Before she could answer, Mat said, "How about you tell us first whether you killed–" He faltered a moment. He'd been about to say they were guards at the mine but stopped himself and started again. "Did you kill the two men outside the mine the other night?"

I was looking at him like he was crazy. I shifted the same look onto Rosario. "Is he for real? Use one of your damned algorithms, Mat! In the first place, why the hell would I kill two random guys outside your mine? And in the second place, surely Rosario has told you we were having dinner at Nacho's that night!" I sat back slowly, shaking my head. "What the hell is going on here?"

Lady Angela sighed loudly. "This is becoming very silly. Harry, you are allowing your imagination to run away with you, and you, Rosario, should really not have allowed things to get to this point."

"I didn't imagine four men trying to kill me this afternoon, Lady Angela."

She dismissed the comment with a flutter of her fingers. "Oh, come now. You know perfectly well kidnappings happen almost routinely in South America. We represent a perfectly legitimate syndicate who have invested a very considerable sum of money in a perfectly legitimate mining and development corporation. We are not about to jeopardize that investment by ordering a *hit,* as you call it, on a travel writer. I *really* think we need to get our heads out of the clouds and stop talking nonsense."

She was good. I had to smile and nod. She had class and style, and she was a cool customer.

"Good to hear somebody talking sense."

"What is it you want to know about us, Harry?" It was Lady Angela again. "We have absolutely nothing to hide. But we do have very legitimate concerns about what can happen to the company if we do not keep a low profile for the next few years."

"Okay." I spread my hands. "To a guy like me who has seen the ugly underbelly of the third world, kidnapping, murder, slavery, drug trafficking on a massive scale..." I gave a small shrug. "It's stuff that goes on. It happens. I have seen it too often to be naïve about it. So I find when I get here that my hotel owner hates me with a real vengeance, and I am curious about why. When I ask her, I get the usual spiel about the United States exploiting the poor, and the CIA and all that bullshit."

I paused a moment to read their faces. They had frozen the moment I used the word *slavery*.

I pushed on. "So I start to notice things about the village." I moved my right leg a few inches forward so I had easy access to my knife. "And I notice there are no kids. Zero. No children. The school is closed. So I ask around. I ask the village people, the women of childbearing age, you know? And they tell me the children have all been taken to the school at the mine. You want to explain that to me?"

Kit had started laughing. Nigel had taken his cue and was laughing into his drink. Lady Angela was gazing at Kit, and her face said she was amused.

"This is," he started, then rectified, shaking his head. "Argentina is making strides, great strides—don't be offended by what I am going to say, Rosario, but in many, many places, the mentality is still third world. And this, *this*, is what you get when you try to help these people by providing them with services they could never otherwise even dream of."

Lady Angela said, "We built them a school and employed teachers of a standard that you might expect at the best private schools in Buenos Aires. Rosario helped us with the interviewing process. Didn't you, darling? The families who work at the mine live on a very cute, comfortable sort of suburb on site, and the kids go to school there. We offered the families in the village – all the neighboring villages and settlements - the opportunity of having their kids board at the school at the mine. They all *jumped* at the chance. What did you think?" She threw back her head and laughed outrageously. "That we were using child slaves?"

They all laughed. I waited till they had finished, then asked her, "Have you ever seen a child slave?"

The laughter stopped. She said, "Of course not."

"Why of course? I have. Six, seven, eight years old, emaciated, starving, expendable. In pain and distress. It's not funny. When you see them, you don't feel like laughing."

"I'm sure, but dear Harry, we have no child slaves here, and there is absolutely no need for you to come galloping to the rescue on your white charger. Come with us tomorrow to see the mine and the processing plant. You can see the school and the children and the parents and put your mind at rest. All we will ask you is to sign a nondisclosure agreement to cover us for the next five years. Agreed?"

I told her we were agreed, and she threw back her head in an extravagant gesture and said, "Thank God! Can we now please have dinner and get drunk!"

And that was what they did, the four of them, demonstrating that the world was their playground and nothing was important enough to worry them. I relaxed and pretended to get drunk with them, but I watched them and studied them with interest. They were intelligent, funny, original thinkers who didn't buy the codes and the rules set down by society. Society didn't own them, they seemed to say; they owned society. Kit told stories about Congress and the Senate that were fascinating and hilarious. Nigel was a billionaire who was not just an inspired investor who could read the market like a book; he was a patron of the arts with a sincere love and deep understanding of opera. Mat, when he got drunk and relaxed, proved to be not just a genius in the field of IT and artificial intelligence but a profound philosophical thinker with mind-bending concepts about what constituted consciousness and intelligence. And Lady Angela Liu was beautiful, brilliant, and witty and held all the others on a leash.

And what I had to keep reminding myself was that these funny, likeable people were the enemy. They were dangerous and ruthless, and somewhere inside their minds, a faculty had failed to develop. It was a faculty that defined the difference between demons and humans, a faculty I had seen present in the most ruthless of soldiers and warriors and absent in the most apparently human of doctors, lawyers, and accountants. It was a faculty we called compassion or sometimes simply kindness.

It was not here. Among all the wit, intelligence, and achievement, it was not present.

We dined superbly, with the best wine Argentina had to offer, with superb mountain trout and succulent spring lamb. We followed that with a world-class selection of cheeses, Napoleon brandy, a ten-year-old Macallan, and a twenty-one-year-old Bushmills. Throughout, Rosario was quiet, allowing the Four Stooges to hold the floor. She didn't get drunk. Her roll was clear. She was the housekeeper. She made sure the gang had everything they needed.

At one a.m., I told them, "Ladies, gentlemen, it has been a fascinating evening." I turned to Rosario. "The food and wine were superb, thank you so much, and I hope to see you all at some point tomorrow morning for our visit to the factory." Addressing Rosario again, I said, "Will you call me?"

She stood. "I'll drive you to the hotel."

I was about to tell her it wasn't necessary, but Lady Angela Liu waved her hand at us.

"Go on, you kids. Go and have fun. We'll have a nightcap, eh, boys, and tuck ourselves up!"

They all laughed, and Rosario took my arm and led me through the spacious living room and out to the front of the house. There was a moon, almost full, lingering over the horizon in the east, turning the sky turquoise and somehow giving what few sounds there were a muffled echo. She opened the driver's door of the Mercedes and said, "You're a good actor."

She climbed in, and I got in the passenger seat beside her. She said, "Anyone who wasn't counting your drinks would swear you were drunk."

I shrugged. "Why spoil the party? They were having fun."

She spun the car and waited at the gate while it opened. "Were you?"

"I wasn't there to have fun, Rosario. You know that."

She pulled out, and we drove slowly through the moonlit village. "You were there to spy."

"Isn't that what they were doing to me? They were spying on

me, and I was spying on them, and you – you were the facilitator."

She didn't say anything more until we pulled up outside the hotel. Then she sat staring ahead of her, up the old, dilapidated road. I reached for the handle, but she said, "I don't believe you are a journalist." I paused, and she turned to look at me. "Not a travel writer, not an investigative reporter. That wasn't training or muscle memory this afternoon. When you killed those men, you knew exactly what you were doing."

I gave a small, humorless laugh. "Are you an expert in training and muscle memory now?" I gave another small laugh and shook my head. "You know what blows my mind? What everybody focuses on about today is how I reacted. Nobody is asking the obvious question. Who were those guys? Do you know why that is, Rosario?"

She didn't answer. She just watched me with moonlight bathing her face. I leaned toward her and whispered, "Because you all already know who they were and why they were trying to kill me."

I opened the door. Her voice stopped me again as I was about to get out. "They tried to kill me too."

"Are you sure? They were holding you, babe, but they had a gun to my head."

I climbed out and closed the door. I was surprised to see her get out the other side. She came around the car and grabbed the lapels of my jacket. Her voice was barely a whisper.

"Harry, I need to talk to you."

"So talk."

She put her finger on my lips. "Not here. Be quiet."

I turned and opened the door for her. She went in ahead of me. There was no one on reception at that time, and I followed her up the stairs to the galleried landing. At my door, as I fitted the key, she put her fingers to her lips. I opened the door, and again she went in ahead of me.

Inside, she made her way to the bedside table, where she

picked up the receiver of the old telephone, placing her purse on the hook to keep it depressed, unscrewed the earpiece, and showed it to me. The bug was there, small and round, like a watch battery, but unmistakable. For a moment, I wondered if Carla knew it was there, but that was a problem for the next day. I picked up my tooth mug and said, "You want a nightcap, one for the road?"

"Yeah, that would be nice."

I opened the whiskey, poured a measure, and said, "Here – ah shit!" I poured the drink into the earpiece. It crackled and smoked. Then I reached down and pulled the telephone cable out of the wall. After that, I stepped up close, pulled her to me, and breathed in her ear, "Are there any others?"

I felt her tremble, and she slipped her arms around my waist under my jacket. "No," she said. "Now nobody can hear us scream."

ELEVEN

THE LUMINOUS GREEN DIGITS ON THE CLOCK SAID IT was four-thirteen in the morning. The room was dark, but the small balcony outside the open French doors was glowing softly in the moonlight. There was also a soft glow emanating from the bathroom. The door was not quite closed. I lay still and quiet, listening to the sounds.

At first, they were the sounds you expect from a bathroom at a quarter past four in the morning. But after that, there was the zipper on my toilet bag, and a while after that, the two drawers under the sink, then silence.

The bathroom door eased open, and a broad oblong of light spread across the wall opposite. Then the light flipped off. I allowed my breathing to slow and catch a little on my soft pallet.

I sensed rather than heard her move across the room. Then her presence loomed dark in front of me, between me and the balcony, and I smelled her perfume close to my face. I forced myself to relax, opened my eyes a fraction, and waited for the movement, for the sudden lunge.

It didn't come. There was movement, but it was movement away from me. I opened my eyes and watched her naked shadow move across the room back toward the bathroom.

I slipped silently out of bed and went after her. I stood in the bathroom doorway and leaned on the jamb as, in the semi-darkness, she placed the scissors back in the drawer. She saw me and jumped, gasped, and stepped back. For a moment, her eyes registered terror.

"What were you going to do, Rosario? Cut my hair, like Delilah did with Samson?"

Her voice was barely a whisper. "No..."

"You never killed anyone before, huh? It's harder than it looks."

"No."

"Who gave you the order, Rosario?"

She was staring into my face, swaying slightly. I could see the tears in her eyes. "I don't want..." She trailed off. "I can't do it. It's not..." She was giving her head little shakes. "I can't."

I took her gently by the shoulders and turned her to face me. "Listen to me. You don't have to. Who gave you the order? Who told you to do it?"

"Nelson."

I frowned. "Nelson told you to do it?"

Again the small shake of her head. "No, Nelson is my uncle." She stared into my face. Her cheeks were wet, reflecting the soft light of the moon. "My mother's brother."

"What are you telling me, Rosario? He's your uncle?"

She came close to me, put her arms around me with her head on my chest, and began to weep. I could feel her skin against mine, her tears wet on my chest. She said, "Papa," and kept repeating it. "Papa, papa, papa..."

I led her back to the bedroom and sat her on the bed. I poured her a shot of whiskey and made her take a sip. She shuddered, but it seemed to settle her. I put my arm around her and encouraged her to take another sip.

When she was ready I asked her, "What are you trying to tell me, Rosario?"

"My father is ill." She spoke to her hands folded in her lap. "He has Alzheimer's. My uncle put him in a clinic..."

She trailed off. I said, "Don't tell me. The clinic is attached to the mine."

"It is a clinic in Coneta, ten miles outside Catamarca. It belongs to a medical consortium which is owned by Hunt Holdings."

"Nigel's holdings company."

"Yes. They own me. Everything my father did for me, everything I have worked for, is nothing. I belong to them."

"And they told you to kill me."

"Yes. I must make it seem that Carla has done it."

I frowned. "Why? What have they against Carla?"

She closed her eyes and shook her head. Her voice was barely audible. "Nothing... You try to rape her, she defends herself..."

"Sweet Jesus."

"Now they will kill my father to punish me."

"No." I shook my head. "We'll find a way."

She stared miserably into my face. "How...?"

I stood and went for my cell. I dialed, and it rang three times before he answered. Even at that time of the morning, he sounded wide awake.

"Harry, a problem?"

"Yeah, a slight change of plan. Before proceeding, I need to collect somebody from a clinic in Coneta."

"What is this?"

"You got a minute?"

"Of course. It's half past four in the morning, Harry."

I outlined the dinner for him. "Rosario brought me back to the hotel and stayed. At just after four, she got up. She thought I was asleep. She went to get the scissors from the bathroom. She had been ordered to kill me, but she didn't. She put the scissors back in the bathroom drawer. When I confronted her, she told me her dad was diagnosed with Alzheimer's and is confined to a clinic. The clinic belongs to Nigel Hunt, one of the guys at dinner last night. So they pretty much own her. Even so, she pulled back from killing me."

"Have you thought this through? Could it be a trap?"

"Sure, but it's hard to see what benefits it could bring. What can they do in Coneta that they can't do here?"

He grunted. "This is beyond our brief, Harry. You are not Sir Galahad."

"Yeah, but I'm not James Bond, either. This whole job is beyond my brief. I don't investigate. I execute."

"All right."

"And if that executing is to have any meaning, then it has to be done right. Otherwise I become the monster I am supposed to kill."

"All right, Harry. Take it easy. How do you want to do this?"

"Go and get him. Can we jam their phones?"

"Probably. It's short notice, but I'll see what we can do."

I hung up. She was sitting on the bed in the darkness, with the moonlight reflected in her eyes. They were fixed on me, staring.

"So they were right," she said. "You are a spy."

I shook my head and started pulling on my jeans. "I am not a spy."

"You were talking to..." She trailed off. "That was not an editor."

"Get dressed. If you want your father to live, you need to move." I pulled on my boots and shrugged into a shirt. "Once they realize you have not killed me, your father and you will have hours to live. So you'd better get your ass in gear."

She didn't move. She sat staring. I watched her as I strapped on the Fairbairn and Sykes and shoved the Sig into my waistband.

"You regretting your decision?" I said. She didn't answer. "You fancy your chances better than the four guys who stopped us on the road or the two guys outside the factory the other night?"

"That was you."

"Yeah, that was me. Now if you are smart, you will get dressed in a hurry and let me save your life and your dad's. If you are stupid, you will try to keep your dad in prison and yourself a slave."

She started pulling on her clothes. I opened the door, and we moved silently down the stairs to the reception area. In the entrance hall, I told her, "Give me the keys." She handed me the fob, and I pressed the button to open the doors. They flashed and bleeped loudly in the dark silence. I said, "Go and get behind the wheel."

She crossed the sidewalk, opened the door, and slid into the driver's seat. It took only a matter of seconds: two pairs of running feet and a hoarse rasp, "Hey! Hey! Rosario! Lo hiciste? Esta hecho?"

She opened the door and looked back as they approached. They were medium height, probably both in their thirties. One of them had a cigarette between his fingers in his right hand. He was balding and had a moustache. The other was skinny and had black hair slicked back. They stood either side of the open door, where she was looking up at them. The guy with the cigarette said, "Podemos subir?" My basic Spanish told me he was asking if they could go up.

Her hesitation was a fraction of a second before she said, "Si, esta hecho."

By then, I was up behind them. I drove the fighting knife deep into the smoking man's back, just below his left shoulder blade. A spasm made him shudder, and he leaned on the Merc, saying, "Ah...ah..." But by that time, I had let go of the knife and smashed a right hook into the other guy's temple. He was going to fall, but I wasn't sure he was dead, so I took a hold of his greasy hair in my left hand and smashed the blade of my hand into his windpipe. I shoved him forward so he fell face down. I put him out of his rasping misery by stamping on the back of his neck.

I wrenched open the door and snapped, "Get in the passenger seat."

She scrambled out, stifled a small scream as she stepped over the bodies, and ran around to the passenger side. By the time she was in and slamming the door, I had the engine running. I pulled away quietly and took as circuitous route as I could through the village, but there was no way of avoiding driving past her ranch on the outskirts of the town, because it was on the only road there was. It was a forlorn hope, but I killed the lights before driving past and kept the speed below fifty to avoid any growl from the engine.

A mile past the house, I could see no lights in my rearview. A real pro could follow me with his headlights off, but what I had seen so far was not real pro. They had expected a journalist who might be a problem. They had not expected a problem who might be a journalist. But that was what they had gotten.

I put the headlights on, took the car to a hundred, and kept it at that speed until we hit the bends and began to descend into the valley. There was no sign of any lights behind us, and however professional a tail was, keeping up at a hundred MPH with no headlights was a tall order. I began to feel maybe we had gotten away unseen.

For now.

The two guys I'd taken down outside the hotel would be expected to check in sooner or later, besides which, when the hotel and the street started stirring at seven or eight in the morning, the bodies would be seen and reported, and then there would be a full-on hunt. Rosario broke in on my thoughts suddenly.

"They will say you have abducted me."

I glanced at her. The steep, wooded hills slipped by silently outside in the moonlight.

"Maybe. Whatever they gain from being able to use the cops as resources, they lose by risking a police investigation."

"That is ridiculous. Why would the police investigate them?"

"You don't know?" I studied her face a moment before taking the next hairpin. "I almost believe you."

"I don't know what you're talking about."

"You're unreal. Why the hell do you think they ordered you to kill me, Rosario? Come on! You're a lawyer, for crying out loud! Use your brain!"

Her face contracted with anger. "Because you were spying on them! They stand to lose billions of dollars! I don't condone it, but that is their reason! You really think the Argentine police will listen to your version of events rather than theirs?"

I drove in silence for a while, concentrating on the tight bends as we sped down toward the valley. I was turning things over in my head, trying to reach a conclusion that eluded me every time I reached for it. Finally I asked her, "Where do you think the kids are?"

"You asked that last night."

"You buy what they said? Knowing what you know about them, knowing what they did to your father..."

"Please stop." She said it with no apparent feeling in her voice. "It's different. They need to control me. I deal with legal and administrative issues, I could be bribed, bought... You don't know what it's like doing business in Latin America..." Her voice trailed off.

We came out of the canyon, and the road leveled off and straightened. Ahead, the first hint of gray was touching the eastern horizon. I hit the gas, and we surged to a hundred and twenty toward the Chumbicha intersection. I screamed through with a minor fishtail, and then it was an empty, almost straight road for thirty-five miles. We covered it in fifteen minutes. Rosario sat rigid in her seat, with her eyes fixed on the road ahead.

"You think it's different?" I said. "Let me tell you what I think. I think there are mothers in the village of Poman who have not seen their children since they were taken to the school at the mine. I think there are mothers in all those small villages on Nelson McCormack's land, whose husbands work for the mine, who have not seen their children since they were taken to the school at the mine. But all those Indian villages and settlements up in the mountains, the ones who are not entered on any census? I think they are different. I think they see their kids every day, because they, the mothers, the fathers and the children, all work at the mine and the processing plant. Along with the kids from Poman and all the other villages. Because there is no school, and you know it."

"Stop it. I don't believe that."

"Have you seen it? Have you seen this wonderful school? *Have you?*"

She didn't answer. I began to slow. Up ahead, there was a turning to the left. A sign by the side of the road said, *Clínica Jardín de Edén*.

I dropped to third and took the corner, then cruised along among the trees that fringed the road. After a couple of minutes, we came to a tall iron gate on the left flanked by ten-foot walls. There was only one camera immediately visible, and that was focused on the gate itself. I figured security at that kind of clinic was all about keeping people in rather than keeping them out.

I stopped and noticed, thirty yards up the road, concealed by the shadow of the trees across from the clinic wall, the shadow of a vehicle. My cell pinged.

We are thirty-five yards ahead of you. Join us here.

I pulled forward and tucked the Mercedes under the trees in front of what I could now see was an Ineos Grenadier.

I turned to Rosario. "Give me your cell." She reached in her purse and handed it over. "Stay here. Don't move."

I climbed out and saw two figures emerge from the truck and approach. They stopped before their faces became visible. Then I heard the brigadier's voice.

"I think you've blown the mission, Harry."

TWELVE

CHUCK STOOD BESIDE THE BRIGADIER. IN THE HALF-light, neither of them looked happy.

I said, "Why? They were planning on killing me last night. As far as they're concerned, I'm dead."

A small breeze rustled the leaves and made me shudder. The brigadier shook his head. "Until they discover, in the next hour or two, that you and Rosario have disappeared. They'll start shutting down the operation, and the big prizes will be on the next air taxi back to the United States."

"No." It was my turn to shake my head. "These guys are not stupid. They will deduce correctly that the first thing Rosario is going to do is come for her dad. And they will do two things. They will phone to see if she has come, and they will send a car after us. They will all four be aware of one, overriding factor. As long as I am loose, they cannot go back to the States. I make the facts available to an American federal prosecutor, and they are fucked six ways to Sunday. But as long as they are south of the border, they have corruption and their vast wealth on their side."

He grunted. Chuck looked down at him and frowned. "It makes sense, sir."

"All right," he said, "but everything hinges on how we handle this part of the operation. What are you thinking?"

I took five minutes to tell him. He nodded, and we all went and got in the Merc, then did a U-turn and pulled up in front of the gate. There I turned to Rosario.

"We are going to get out and buzz reception. We are here on behalf on Nelson McCormack and Nigel Hunt -"

"They will call to confirm."

"Not at this time of the morning, they won't. And even if they try, they won't get through." She hesitated, and I pressed her. "It's the one play we've got. Stop wasting time."

I got out, and she came after me. I heard the two rear doors slam and knew the brigadier and Chuck were with us. We approached the gate, and she pressed the button on the intercom. After a moment, an image of Rosario and me with two indistinct figures behind us appeared on the small, slightly warped silver screen. A voice crackled, "Si? Quien es?"

"Venimos de parte de Nelson McCormack y Nigel Hunt, para ver a un paciente. Es urgente."

She turned to me. "He asks who we are. I said we come on behalf of Nelson and Nigel to see a patient. It is urgent."

There was a delay of maybe thirty seconds that felt more like an hour. Then the gate buzzed and began to roll slowly back. Rosario and I pushed inside with the brigadier just behind us. Chuck climbed back in the car and followed us up the drive to the main door.

It was a large, rectangular, Spanish colonial building in sage green and white. Three shallow steps rose to the main entrance. I ran up these with Rosario and the brigadier on my heels.

The reception was spacious, with a checkerboard floor and a mahogany staircase rising to the upper floor and passages branching off right, left, and ahead. There was a reception desk on the right, and behind it a young man with wire spectacles and a face that asked no questions and did what it was told. A tag on his white coat said his name was Eugenio Rojas.

The brigadier took up a position by the door and looked more menacing than you'd expect. Rosario and I approached the desk, and Chuck came in and stood right behind us, looking more menacing than the brigadier. Rosario drew breath, but I cut her short.

"Eugenio Rojas, you speak English?"

"Yes, sir."

"You know who Nigel Hunt is?"

"Yes, sir."

"He owns this place. He owns you. I represent Mr. Hunt, you understand me? So when you talk to me, you are talking to Nigel Hunt. When I talk to you, Nigel Hunt is talking to you. Are we clear?"

He'd gone the color of candle wax. He nodded once. "Yes, sir."

"Do you know who Nelson McCormack is?"

"Yes sir."

"His brother is here, a very sick man. His name—"

I turned to Rosario. She said, "Jesus Fuentes."

"His name is Jesus Fuentes. We need you to bring him out here now. We are in a hurry."

"Sir, I need to telephone for authorization. The telephones are not working, it is so early…"

He trailed off because the brigadier had come closer, and Chuck had leaned on the desk with both hands, allowing his jacket to fall open, revealing the Smith and Wesson 29 he carried under his arm. His voice sounded like he was grinding gravel with his vocal cords.

"Did I mention we were in a hurry?"

"Yes, sir."

"Is there some part of that you don't understand?"

"No."

Chuck smiled in a way that was disturbing on many levels and said, "Show me the way. I will help you."

Eugenio looked at me. I nodded. "It's best to do what he

says." I leaned forward with a confidential smile. "I'll tell Nigel you did everything by the book." I winked. He looked vaguely nauseous and led Chuck up the mahogany stairs to the upper floor. Rosario moved to follow, but I gripped her arm.

"You stay with me. You don't say another word to anyone, and you especially do not speak in Spanish. Understood?"

Her eyes said she wanted to tear my face off, but she stayed.

Five minutes later, Eugenio appeared on the stairs and trotted down. Behind him was Chuck carrying in his arms what looked at first like a loose sack of bones. Rosario flushed, put her hands to her mouth, and stifled a small cry. The distress was genuine. There was no mistaking it.

She moved to Chuck, holding out her hands to the old man. I heard him rasp, "Rosario..."

"Papa!"

"Que pasa? Que ocurre?"

Chuck, the brigadier, and Rosario moved quickly out into the predawn. They walked past the Mercedes, and I knew they were headed for the Range Rover. I stepped up close to Eugenio and spoke quietly.

"Do you know what Nigel Hunt and Nelson McCormack will do to you if they believe you collaborated in this rescue?" He went ashen and began to tremble. I said, "They will have you killed. Now I am going to do you a favor. You give me all the video footage of our arrival and any other footage from reception, the corridor, or the bedroom, and then I will tell you what to do to save your ass. Okay?"

He nodded, hurried behind the desk, fumbled with a hard drive, and produced a pen drive. I took it. "This is everything? It's for your own good. Your life depends on it."

"Yes." He was sweating profusely.

"Okay. Listen carefully. Three men in ski masks shot out the lock, knocked you unconscious, and took Mr. Fuentes. That simple. Understood?"

"Yes."

"Hit me."

"*What?*"

"Hit me. Come on! I'm in a hurry!"

"No!"

I smacked him hard in the jaw to ensure a good, swollen bruise. Then I stamped on his hand to make it look like he'd hit me real hard defending the clinic. Then I ran down the drive, Chuck blew out the latch on the gate with his Dirty Harry gun, and we jumped in the truck and sped sedately away from the clinic.

Speeding sedately is something you can only do in a Range Rover.

The brigadier was at the wheel. In the back, Rosario had her arms around her dad and was crying softly. The brigadier's voice broke in on my thoughts.

"I don't suppose you have given any thought to where we are going to take Mr. Fuentes and his daughter."

"It was all a little last minute, sir."

He was quiet for a moment before saying, "Last-minute plans are the ones that get people killed, Harry."

"I know, but there was no other alternative. Getting killed was what I was trying to avoid." I gave a small shrug and added, "It has at least the advantage of being unexpected for the other side."

"Your theory is that they will stay put and start searching for you as though you were attempting to flee the country."

We had reached the intersection. Ahead, the sky was turning gray and pink. A couple of cars passed. They had their headlights on, but they didn't need them in the grainy, pink light.

Left would take us into Catamarca. Right would take us south, skirting the mountains toward Cordoba and La Rioja. It would also take us, with another right turn, back to Poman. He turned right. He drove at a steady pace and glanced in the mirror at Rosario.

"Rosario Fuentes?"

Her voice came from the back. It sounded damp. "Yes."

"I am going to leave you with friends. They will give you travel documents for you and your father to travel to the United States. There you will be met at the airport and taken care of. You understand?"

She was silent for a moment. Then, "Of course, but..."

"If you stay here, your life is at risk, and so is that of your father. We don't want anything bad to happen to you, but I won't pretend there are no strings attached."

There was a hint of irony in her voice when she said, "Of course."

"We believe the mine outside Poman is employing slave labor, and particularly child slaves. Is that something you approve of?"

There was absolutely no inflection or emotion in his voice, and somehow that made the question shocking. I heard her gasp. "Of course not! But that is absurd!"

"I am not asking you to assess the intelligence, Ms. Fuentes. We have experts who do that. I am asking you if you approve of it."

"Of course I don't."

"Good. Then if we provide you with conclusive evidence, you will have no problem providing us with information about the consortium that has set up the mine."

"If..." She faltered. "If you have conclusive evidence, of course..." She trailed off again, then said, "I have never been to the mine."

She was quiet for a while. Then she spoke with a sudden savagery in her voice. "Again the United States Empire comes marching in! When it was oil, you take control of the Middle East! Now it is lithium, so you march into Argentina with lies about child slaves and conclusive evidence which you manufacture on your CGI computers! You think I don't know what the CIA can do?"

The brigadier let her finish. When she fell silent, he said, "Have you ever met a Saudi prince, Rosario?" She didn't answer. "I'd advise you to do a little research into the various US presidents since Kennedy was assassinated and get clear about who owns whom in the Middle East, Washington DC, and London before you start throwing around accusations. But if I were in your position, working as you do for Liumin Corporation – that is what they are called, isn't it?"

"Yes."

"Working as you do for them and having heard what Harry and I have said, I would want to be very sure there were no children being abused and exploited at that mine. I have to say that right now you seem more concerned about political abstracts and stereotypes than the children from your village." She didn't say anything. He kept his eyes on her in the mirror. "If we are right, how many do you think have died by now? How many are sick, how many have been beaten? Do you know? Do you care? Or are you happy to dismiss the whole idea just because Harry is American and I am English?" Before she could answer, he added, "Let me ask you something, Rosario. What nationality is Kit O'Hanlon? How about Nigel Hunt or Mat Coren? What nationality is Lady Angela Liu? What about other members of the consortium? How many do you know? How many are Argentine?"

She still didn't answer. I noticed he was slowing and pulling over to the side of the road. He stopped and turned in his seat to look at her.

"Remind me why we are here, Rosario. Remind me why you are holding your father in your arms. Remind me who put him in that home. Your uncle, right? And what nationality is he? Morality is not a product of nationality, Ms. Fuentes. Remember that when you sit safe and secure in your new house in the States while the children die in the mine owned by your uncle."

"Enough!"

"Are you sure?"

Ahead, through the windshield, I could see two Blackwing Caddies approaching. I said, "We have company."

"I invited them." The brigadier glanced at me, then turned back to Rosario. "These people are going to take you to the American Embassy, and from there, they are going to fly you to the States. They will want to ask you questions. Will you cooperate?"

The two sports sedans pulled up across the road from us. Rosario jerked her head at me. "What is he going to do?"

"He is going to make sure no more children get abused or enslaved."

"I will go with him. I will see it with my own eyes. If it is true, I will talk to your men in Washington."

He turned to me. I shook my head. "No way. It will get us both killed."

She interrupted. "No, I return with my father alone or I return with you. But I have to see this with my own eyes. We can work it out. We can prepare an explanation for them. I can say you are dead; I killed you. But I go back."

I shook my head again. "It's impossible. They know by now your father was snatched."

The lead Cadillac driver's window slid down. A guy in shades called over, "You have thirty seconds and we are going."

The brigadier gave him the thumbs up, then he and Chuck swung down with the old man. Chuck carried him to the rear Caddy, and the brigadier tossed me the fob.

"The Range Rover is yours. Do what you have to do. We're out of time." To Rosario, he said, "Your father will be waiting for you. Try to stay alive. He needs you. When you are satisfied, make your way to the embassy."

Then he was gone, and the sedans were accelerating away toward Catamarca, where the molten edge of the sun was bleeding over the horizon. I climbed out of the passenger seat, went around the hood, and got behind the wheel. Rosario took the difficult route between the front seats to get in the passenger side. When she was seated, I scowled at her.

"Congratulations, you just sentenced us both to death. You want to tell me what your big plan is?"

"Yes," she said. "When I have thought of it."

THIRTEEN

Sudden hot anger surged in my belly, and I turned on her.

"What you just did was stupid, Rosario! It is not funny, and it's not smart! Those people were trying to help you and your father! *I* was trying to help you both! I could have left you for Angela Liu to deal with. I could have left you tied up and gagged in my room! But I tried to help you, and what do I damn well get for it? A death sentence hung around my neck because you believe those bastards have some kind of humanity in them! It was *stupid!*"

There was a kind of loud, ringing silence in the cab after I stopped shouting. She sat watching me. I took a deep breath and thumped the steering wheel gently with the heel of my hand.

"This is what we are going to do. We are going to find a cheap hostel, and we are going to book a room. You are going to stay in the hostel and wait for me. Tonight I will go and do what I have to do, and tomorrow we head back to the States. Me on a plane and you via the embassy."

"No."

"Don't start this, Rosario."

"I am sorry."

I felt the heat rise to my face again. "Look! There are just two ways you can see the kids. One is by going and talking to your uncle or his partners, in which case you will be killed and probably tortured first. Or you can come with me into the mine, where you will get killed and probably get me killed too. You are putting the whole operation in jeopardy! Don't you see that?"

"What I see, Harry, is that if you try to get into the mine and free the children, you, and probably the children, will get killed."

I answered with a touch of bitterness, "We are professionals, Rosario. We know what we are doing."

"You are also one man on your own."

"That's how I work best."

"I have seen that," she said quietly. "But there are hundreds of people working at the mine. You cannot beat them all. You need to get to the managers, and for that, you need to get to my uncle and the representatives of the corporation. There is only one way you can do that."

"Yeah, I go there tonight and break into the -"

"Now you are being stupid. You know perfectly well that by tonight, the house will be crawling with security."

I was beginning to feel curious. I frowned and said, "So what are you suggesting?"

"You use me as a hostage."

"*What?* You're out of your mind! They *want* you dead."

"Exactly. Especially by this afternoon, they will want me silenced permanently. And you will not be threatening to kill me. You will be threatening to hand me over to the Federal Bureau of Investigation. If everything you and your boss believe is true, they will want me dead. So what I am suggesting is that you telephone them, threaten them with handing me over, and use me as a hostage so that they will show you the children at the mine and prove to me that it's true. We will record the conversation and hand it not only to the FBI, but also to the Argentine authorities."

"Slow down!" I said. "I need to think this through. We need to hole up, and I need to think."

"You know the last place they will look for you?"

"We are not going back to the hotel."

"No, sixty miles or so past Poman, there is a town called Andalgalá. It is a large town with tourists and several hotels. The main access is on Route 48 from Concepción. But in this different car, we can approach on 46, passing Poman, and nobody will expect it. They will assume we have gone for Buenos Aires or another major city to get a flight. Or driving to Chile."

It made a lot of sense. I nodded. "Okay, we'll head up. You call and make a reservation." As an afterthought, I added, "Ask if they have the honeymoon suite available." She gave me that *Are you kidding me?* look. I almost smiled as I pulled away and did a U-turn to head back up the mountain. "It's a lesson I learned a long time ago. Nobody ever suspects the people in the five-star hotel, the first-class compartment, or the honeymoon suite."

She made a face and pulled out her cell.

We drove in silence through the dawn and early morning. I drove fast, wanting to get away from the vast, open spaces where a moving Range Rover stood out like a beacon on the long, empty roads. Wanting also to arrive at a quiet, anonymous place where I could think. I knew what Rosario had said made sense, but it also rang alarm bells in my mind, and however I moved the pieces around, I couldn't see why.

We arrived in Andalgalá by mid morning. It was bigger than I expected, and we spent an hour on and around the main street, Calle Núñez del Prado, buying a couple of suitcases and clothes to go in them. Then we headed for the hotel.

It was a sprawling one-story building in the Spanish style with corrugated terracotta tiles on the gabled roofs and the walls painted a kind of adobe yellow. There was something attractive about the place, despite – or perhaps because of –the six acres of shambling, unkempt land that surrounded it.

We nosed in through the gate and parked the Range Rover in

the shade of the giant cactus that stood beside the seven steps that led up to the door. As we climbed down from the cab, a guy in a white shirt with a cigarette hanging from the side of his mouth came down. He didn't seem to see us, but he opened the trunk, pulled out our brand-new luggage and carried it up to reception, just behind us.

The inside of the hotel wasn't much different than the outside. It was charming and shabby and slightly melancholy, like it remembered the '60s, when it was young, exotic, and sexy.

We checked in, and the guy with the white shirt and the butt in his mouth carried our cases to a room that had a big, heavy bed, a small annex with a sofa, a coffee table and TV, and an en suite bathroom. I gave him ten bucks, and he grinned, grunted, and left, trailing small clouds of ash.

After that, we showered and changed our clothes and made our way to the restaurant for lunch. The dining room had high ceilings with fans suspended. The walls were the same adobe yellow as the outside, and there were tall, wooden-framed windows that stood open to let in the sunlight and a gentle, fresh breeze. We were alone. There were a couple of tables outside on the lawn, where the only other guests were seated.

A waiter in a bowtie and a burgundy waistcoat brought us a couple of menus. I ordered a couple of martinis, and he went away. I pulled my phone from my pocket and said, "Okay, let's do this. What's the number?"

Her eyes darted over my face for a moment before she closed them and said, "I'm scared."

"Good. You should be."

"Is this going to work? Are we going to be okay?"

Her cheeks had colored and her breathing had accelerated. I could see her chest rising and falling. I injected some conviction I didn't feel into my voice and said, "Yes. Be smart, don't do any more crazy stuff like you did this morning, and we'll be okay."

For a moment, she didn't say anything. Then she took a deep

breath and recited a number. I put it in my phone and said, "Who is this?"

"Angela."

"She runs the show, right?"

"I believe so. There is a consortium, but I believe she has the biggest block of shares." She hesitated, then added, "Between the four of them and my uncle, they have a controlling share."

I smiled. "Are they all as crazy as these four?"

She echoed the smile but with not much feeling. "I haven't met any of the others. Angela told me they had made a point of seeking out investors who thought out of the box, who were visionary about the future. She said..." She trailed off, like she was trying to remember. "She said people like Zuckerberg, Musk, Ellison, and others I don't remember, these people she said owned the future. She said they had to be a bit crazy in order to have a different vision, and these were the people she wanted investing in lithium. She said artificial intelligence was the future, and lithium would drive AI."

I sighed. "Crazy as a soup sandwich. And this is the future. God help us."

I dialed. While it was ringing, the waiter brought us our martinis, and as he was leaving, Angela's voice snapped, "Yes!"

I smiled at Rosario, who looked pale. "Good afternoon, Angela. How are you feeling this morning? A little hung over?"

There was a long silence, then, "Who is this?"

I laughed. "Come on! You don't recognize me? I am wounded. Not physically, of course, I managed to avoid that, but emotionally, in my heart." I chuckled loudly enough for her to hear. "My *metaphorical* heart. The other, organic one is just fine. I know you'll be relieved to hear that."

"What do you want, Mr. Bauer?"

"Me? I just want us to be friends, Angela. We got along so well last night. You introduced me to such interesting people. I thought Nigel and Mat were such interesting people, and the senator, Kit O'Hanlon. Of course I had seen him around in DC. But you know who I really took to? Rosario. She was a *killer*."

"You made your point, Bauer. I am asking you what you want."

"Well, Angela, it's not so much a matter of what I want as what you want. Me? I'm just a soldier of fortune. Que será será. Know what I'm saying? But you? You and Kit and Mat and Nigel. You have so much in the balance, so much to gain, and so much to lose."

"Will you ever get to the point?"

I laughed. "Oh, a woman of your intelligence, Angela? I thought you'd be there well ahead of me. By the way, Rosario sends her regards. She'd tell you personally, but she's a little tied up right now. You know," I laughed again, "with rope and stuff. So as I know you guys are based in the United States, I thought I'd reach out and ask if..." I paused a moment and then said very deliberately, "...if you'd like to see her in DC. Because, you know, I have taken such a liking to her, I am really looking forward to taking her to DC with me. If not DC, I can think of a place on Broadway in Manhattan where I'd love to take her."

There was another prolonged silence, then, "No, I would not like to see her in DC or New York, Mr. Bauer."

"Harry. Let's be friends, Angela."

"Harry. What would it take for you not to deliver her to the Feds?"

I put the phone on speaker and held it in front of me. "I'm sorry, I am dressing for lunch while I talk to you. What did you say?"

"What would it take, Harry, to convince you not to hand her over to the FBI?"

"Yeah, see, I've been thinking about that. I give you a price, you make the transfer, I hand over Rosario, and then you not only kill her, you then send some sicario after me too. I don't want to spend the rest of my life looking over my shoulder, you know what I mean?"

"It may be a little late for that."

"No, I don't think so. I think we can reach an understanding that is beneficial to us all." I gave a wolfish laugh and added, "Not for Rosario, right? But for the rest of us."

"I'm fascinated. Do tell."

"For the time being, I hold on to Rosario. Then we are going to do the following. You let me see and photograph the kids you have working at the mine."

"Out of the question."

"Hear me out, baby. Right now, you are not in a position to lay down the law. You let me see the children and document them. Now let me be clear. I want the proof that these kids are being exploited as slaves."

"You must be out of your mind!"

"You may be right. But hear me out. When I have my information, I deposit that somewhere safe, and then you pay me a simple two percent of gross every year. In exchange, I give you Rosario."

Again the long silence. Then, "How do I know that once you have your two percent you won't start demanding more?"

"We'll make a contract with our attorneys that the attaché case containing the information can only be handed over if you and I are both present and sign for it, unless I die of anything other than old age. In which case, it goes directly to the Bureau."

Her voice was savage. "This is ridiculous!"

"That two percent, Angela, gives you all the guarantee that I will play ball. Piss me off or keep me waiting, and I'll be heading for the airport, and in less than twenty-four hours, you'll have the Feds paying visits to all your offices across the USA."

She said more quietly, "It's absurd."

"Fine. It's been nice talking to you, Angela. No doubt we'll be seeing each other after extradition proceedings -"

"Wait. Just give me a minute to think, will you?"

"You have fifty-five seconds left and counting."

"Good Lord, you're a pain in the ass!"

"So I've been told. You're out of options, Angela. You need to have a meeting with your boys. I'll be expecting a call this evening before seven. I don't want you interrupting my dinner. You'd better have some arrangements in place for me to see the mine tomorrow afternoon, sweet cheeks, or you will have a problem. Do we understand each other?"

"Of course we understand each other. I am not a moron! How do I know you haven't sent Rosario on to the States?"

"You don't. But if you're not a moron, neither am I. I am smart enough to realize that my two percent depends on you silencing Rosario."

"All right."

"And Angela, when I set eyes on those kids, you had better not have bathed and showered them and stuck them in some phony schoolroom. I want them as they are, dirty, bruised, and working their little butts off. Understand?"

"I understand, Harry. You'll see them in all their miserable glory."

"I can't wait. Call me on this number, tonight before seven."

I hung up and set the phone between us on the table. Rosario was very quiet, looking down at her hands laid flat on the table.

"How could I have been so stupid?"

"It's not hard. I do it all the time."

She narrowed her eyes at me. "But why? What can they possibly achieve? What purpose..." Her words died away.

"You know the answer to that, Rosario. Profits. You know that for a workforce to run a mine of that size costs hundreds of thousands of dollars, not just in salaries but in taxes and insurance contributions. They'd have had to bring in a lot more investors and settle for a much smaller share of the market. This way, not only does the money go into their pockets instead the works and the IRS, but they get to work these people around the clock. It's not just the kids, it's all those non-census Indians from the villages and settlements too. All free."

"But do they seriously think they can get away with it?"

I shrugged. "You said it yourself, they're crazy. But then again, if I read those bastards right, the medium-term plan is probably once the mine is up and competitive, pin the slavery on Nelson, and Angela and her pals move in, take over his share, ensure oversight and accountability, and take a bigger share of the international market than they'd ever have achieved if they'd been saddled with the burden of proper staffing costs."

"I am so sorry, Harry. I feel so stupid. What do we do now?"

"Now," I said, "we eat."

FOURTEEN

THE CALL CAME AT FIVE P.M. WHEN I WAS CATCHING UP
on sleep I knew I was going to need, and Rosario was sitting in the
chair by the window chewing her lip and picking her fingers. I sat
up and put the phone on speaker.

"Harry."

"Angela."

"I've discussed the matter with my colleagues and, all things
considered, two percent per annum does not seem too steep a
price to pay, and we agree, having you as part of the team, so to
speak, might be the best way to avoid future problems."

"Good."

"However, there is one thing we want from you."

"What's that?"

"If we are going to show you our dark secret, we want to see
yours."

"What are you talking about?"

"We want you to kill Rosario, and we want to film you doing
it. Then that video goes in with the footage of the children."

I looked over at her on the sofa. She'd gone the color and
texture of candle wax.

"That's not a problem. But there is the question of timing. I don't give up Rosario until I have the kids as insurance."

"Yes, I thought of that. We can sort it. You make your movie. We allow you to transmit it to a remote source without jamming it, and simultaneously we film you killing Rosario."

I sighed and rolled my eyes. "This is Nigel's idea, right?"

There was a brief pause. "Yes."

"It's got Nigel written all over it. Did Mat add a few algorithms?"

"Have we got a deal or not?"

"Yeah, whatever. Where do we meet and when?"

"Tomorrow, twelve noon -"

I cut across her. "Later. Three p.m."

I could hear the smile in her voice. "Why, what's wrong with noon?"

"That's none of your goddamn business. Three p.m. or the deal is off."

"Fine, three p.m. at the main gate of the mine. It's on Route 46. Which direction will you be coming from?"

I counted slowly to five. She said, "Harry?"

I knew sooner or later I was going to kill her, and I allowed that knowledge to seep into my voice. "Are we playing games, Angela? Am I coming to this meeting wondering whether you are going to screw me? Am I going to spend the next twenty-two hours in a state of anxiety?"

"No."

"Because that question you just asked me was stupid."

"I apologize."

"It was stupid because it tells me you are trying to figure out where I am."

"I'm sorry, Harry. I was being silly."

"And why would you want to know where I am, Angela? So you can try and track me down and kill me? The way you tried with Rosario? How did that work out for you, Angela?"

"Harry, I apologized. I said I am sorry. I was just playing around."

"Angela, you and your associates want me as a friend. Believe me, you do not want me as an enemy."

"I'm-"

I hung up and dropped the phone on the bed beside me. Rosario had curled up in her chair with her arms crossed over her chest. She was watching me, and there was terror in her eyes.

I studied her face a moment and figured most of the fight had gone out of her.

"You listen to me, Rosario. I am going to tell you what is going to happen. I want no argument. You are going to get in the car and you going to drive nonstop to Buenos Aires. There you are going to go straight to the American Embassy. It's eight hundred miles. You're going to be driving maybe fourteen or fifteen hours. But you have to do it. You can't stop, and you can't rest. Do you understand that? I'll call my boss and tell him to expect you."

"But you, what are you going to do?"

"Nothing you need to know about."

We took five minutes to pack her case. I walked with her out to the car and slung her case in the trunk. I opened the driver's door for her, and she clung to me hard. There was fear and grief in her eyes. I kissed her hard. "Go now. There is no time. I'll catch up with you in New York or DC. You take Route 48 through Concepcion. It adds a little to your trip, but you don't need to pass Poman.

Then Cordoba and Buenos Aires."

"I know, Harry."

She bit her lip, climbed behind the wheel, and a moment later, she was pulling out of the hotel grounds and turning left onto Route 48.

In the reception, I made a show of looking depressed. I was surprised to find it wasn't all that hard a show to put on. The receptionist smiled with a hint of inquiry.

"My wife," I told her. "We're on honeymoon, but she just heard her father is sick."

"Oh, I am sorry to hear that."

"Yeah, we got her the first flight we could. I'll join her tomorrow." She made a sad face, and I gestured toward the door. "She had to take the car. Is there any way I can rent a vehicle through you? I don't know how I'm going to…"

I let the words hang. Her smile was reassuring. "We have a couple of courtesy vehicles, Mr. Bauer."

"That's fantastic. If you can let me have one, I'll drive over and have dinner with a friend tonight. Say six-thirty?"

"Of course."

I made my way back to my room and updated the brigadier.

"Was it her idea to go to Andalgalá?"

I took a second to process the question and smiled. "You bugged the car."

"Of course. Wouldn't you?"

I didn't want to ask, but I couldn't stop myself either. "Where is she now?"

"Headed east on Route 48 toward Concepción."

"You don't trust her, do you, sir?"

"The jury is out. We have insufficient intelligence. These matters are never black and white, Harry. It's not a question of her being a good guy or a bad guy. In the end, it comes down to people protecting their interests. If she's protecting her father and at the same time making a lot of money, after a couple of years, it becomes easy to accept the status quo."

"So why didn't she kill me when she had the chance?"

"Maybe she's infatuated. She is not a hero or a villain, Harry. She is an unfortunate woman who is a victim of circumstances. That is what most people are: unfortunate victims of circumstance."

I grunted. "Will you pick her up?"

"We have a couple of cars on their way. They should intercept her outside Cordoba. I'll call her before they make contact. What's your plan?"

I told him about the phone call I'd had with Angela. "So we've arranged to meet tomorrow afternoon at the entrance to the mine."

"But you'll take action tonight?"

"Yes."

"Good. Keep me posted."

I hung up and looked at my watch. It was closing on six p.m. I had a cold shower and pulled on some dark Levis and a black shirt I'd bought in town. I put the Sig under my arm and pulled on my jacket. My knife was already strapped to my ankle in my boot. Then I strolled down to reception to collect my car.

It was one of those anonimobiles made of plastic and carbon fiber. They are mass produced in France, Germany, and the Far East to give drones a feeling of being special without being different.

I took 46 out of town like I was headed back toward Poman. Dusk was fading. The sun had dipped behind the horizon but had left a ring of fire encircling the world behind the mountains, and everything inside that ring was going dark. The amber glow of the headlights picked out the straight, black ribbon of the road ahead, and pretty soon, I saw the first scattered houses of the village of Saujil and knew I was just ten miles from the entrance to the mine. When I came to the gas station, I came off the road and drove in through the town, as the brigadier had told me to do. I drove slowly until I came to the main square. It was shabby and dilapidated, aside from a white church with a black spire that would have looked more at home in Maine. I turned right and headed out of town along Fray Mamerto Esquiú.

Pretty soon, I was on a road that was listed as Provincial Route 25 but was just an ill-kept dirt track that led through the wilderness to the villages of Rincon, Mischango, and Colana. This dirt track was the only access to these villages, and from what the brigadier had told me when I'd seen him in Catamarca, the villagers did not appear on any census. They were Andes Indians who had their own way of doing things. They didn't need permission from Buenos Aires to exist. They didn't need to be on anybody's list. And Buenos Aires didn't give a damn because nobody in these villages earned enough to pay taxes.

So Provincial Route 25 remained a dirt track in the mountains, and the villages were left in peace.

Until now.

I ground and jolted through the darkness, barely picking out the track with my headlights. At some points, I wondered if the damn car would make it and crawled along at little more than walking pace; at others, the track leveled off and I could make maybe fifteen miles an hour.

After thirty minutes or a little more, the road leveled off, and I found myself pulling into a village of scattered houses that were part shack, part corrugated steel, part bare brick and cement. Each one seemed to have its own orchard behind an improvised fence. There were street lamps, but they were all dark, like the houses. No light filtered from the windows or the doors.

I killed the headlamps and opened the windows. Then I killed the engine. There was total silence. I climbed out of the car and stood looking and listening for any sign of life. After a while, there was a soft rustle up ahead. Slowly, a goat came into focus, standing in the road staring at me. Then behind it a couple more.

I got back in the car and crawled through the village. I saw a pack of dogs, I saw goats and sheep, but I didn't see a single person.

In Mischango and Mutquín, it was the same story. The power had been cut, the villages were in darkness, and the animals were roaming wild. In Mutquín, hunger had started to drive the dogs wild, and I saw two goat carcasses half-eaten in the town square.

The road between these villages, though still just a stretch of dirt through the wilderness of the mountains, seemed to have been more used and was broader and in better condition. So I was able to make better time between Mutquín and Colana, though I stopped short of the last town. The next village after Colana would be Poman. Now it was time to change direction.

Just before the entrance to the village of Colana, there was a broad, deep gully where I figured a powerful stream crashed down from the melting ice in the mountains in the spring. Just before that, there was a small dirt track that trailed down hill to the south through the twisted trees and undergrowth.

I turned into the track, and after five minutes of grinding along the pitted path, I came out onto a small rise where there was a clearing. There I stopped and got out. Far below, maybe five or six miles away across dark woodland, I saw the glow of the processing plant. It was not far now.

I got back in the car and made my way another mile and a half down the track. As I descended, the trees on my right thinned out, replaced by shrubs and rocks, until I finally came to the place the brigadier had told me about. There was a large boulder on my left, beside the stream, and on my right, a small copse of twisted trees. I pulled in beside the boulder, climbed out of the vehicle, and made my way to the far side of the massive rock.

The place wasn't hard to find if you knew what you were looking for. I removed a stack of loose stones and clawed away a couple of inches of soft dirt, and there was a large, military rucksack. I opened it and found inside everything the brigadier had promised, including a collapsible crossbow with a dozen bolts, a speed loader, and an eighty-pound draw weight. In the front pocket, I also found a small tracking device. I checked it briefly, then slung the rucksack on my back, took the crossbow in my hand, and started a quick march across the plain toward the glow of the processing plant. I had no idea at that stage what kind of security I would be facing or whether there would be guards in Jeeps, like the two I had encountered on the first night, patroling the entire perimeter of the mine, or whether they were concentrated primarily around the processing plant. That seemed to me to be the most likely possibility, but at that stage, I simply didn't know.

The ground was covered in small, knotted bushes of something that looked like wild sage. The bushes were just inches apart and made rapid progress difficult, but I got into a rhythm and moved steadily forward. After about twenty-five minutes, the glow from the processing plant had increased enough to be casting the small gnarled trees and bushes into silhouette at the top of a low rise. And that was when I began to see also the silhouette of a tall fence. It was maybe a hundred yards away, supported on large concrete pillars and made of heavy mesh topped with barbed wire or razor wire.

I dropped to the ground and lay motionless for a minute, waiting. Nothing happened, so I removed the rucksack from my back, pulled the binoculars from one of the front pouches, and examined the fence more closely. That was when I saw that it was not one but two fences, separated by a distance of maybe twelve feet. The pillars to which the fence was attached were about two feet in thickness and probably twelve to fifteen feet in height. Each one held a spotlight, but the spotlights were trained inward. I scanned for cameras and found one. It was also focused inward. Security here was designed to keep people in, not out. In theory, that meant I could move closer with no real risk.

It was as that thought passed through my mind that I heard the voices. They weren't loud. They seemed to be engaged in a quiet conversation, but they were growing steadily closer.

FIFTEEN

THERE WERE TWO OF THEM, BOTH IN MILITARY fatigues. They were carrying rifles over their shoulders. A closer look with my binoculars told me they had the distinctive shape of the QBZ-95, the standard issue Chinese PLA assault rifle. But the two guys were not Chinese. They were standard-issue Western mercenaries. Whatever they were, they were not in a hurry, and they were not on any kind of high alert. They looked like they were strolling along discussing their retirement plans. I figured I could help them with that. I figured I'd give them a retirement plan.

I cocked the crossbow, took aim at the farthest of the two guys, allowed half a second for the bolt to reach them, and pulled the trigger. I didn't waste time waiting to see if I'd hit the mark. I cocked the bow again, the bolt slipped into place, and while the second guy was gaping at his friend, who was gripping his chest and sinking to his knees, I put a second bolt right through his spine and his heart.

Eighty pounds of force concentrated onto a razor-sharp tip will drive a bolt clean through a man, and a razor sharp broadhead will cause massive hemorrhaging. These two guys died in seconds, without ever knowing what had happened to them.

I lay motionless, waiting and listening. Nothing happened. So I pulled on my rucksack and sprinted for the nearest concrete pillar. There I dropped to the ground and lay flat. I still heard nothing and saw nothing. Moving fast, I reached into the rucksack and pulled out two pounds of C4. I fixed it to the outside of the pillar where it was not visible from the inside of the compound and inserted a remote detonator. Then at ten yards, I set a directional mine loaded with ball bearings.

Then I sprinted south along the fence. I laid two more C4 packages, fifteen feet apart, and between them, two more directional mines. Finally, I came to the next concrete column. There I set one more C4 package with its corresponding mine and sprinted back into the shadows.

It was as I dropped into the meager cover of some shrubs that I heard the whine of a diesel approaching. It was moving slowly, and as it came into sight, I could see that the driver and his buddy were staring ahead, searching the shadows. It wasn't hard to work out what had happened. The two guys I'd shot hadn't checked in, and these two were checking them out.

I let them get past me, loaded up, and sprinted after them. At fifteen yards, I put a bolt through the driver's back to the left of his spine and hoped for the best. While the Jeep swerved and came to a stop, I loaded up and took my second shot. I got lucky and put the bolt right through his temple.

I now had to cover two miles, and if they were looking for the two guards who hadn't checked in, I was running out of time. I slung my rucksack on the back seat, dragged the dead driver from behind the wheel, put his cap on my head, and turned the Jeep around. I left the passenger in his seat. He looked pretty dead, but at a distance in the dark, he might just look sleepy. I drove not too fast and not too slowly south along the perimeter fence. Along the way, I saw a couple of guys patrolling inside the perimeter. They had dogs, and they didn't look like they were discussing their retirement plans. It was even money whether they would spot the bodies. In my favor was the fact that they would not yet be looking for them; against me was the fact that these guys looked like they were awake, and the bodies would be visible to anyone paying attention.

Either way, there was nothing I could do about it, so I drove on until I reached the southeastern corner of the complex. There I drove into the cover of the sparse woodland the climbed the hills toward Colana. I killed the engine and the lights and pulled the tracking device from the rucksack and checked it again. My second stash was sixty yards to the west, among the trees. I ran.

I took me three minutes to locate it at the foot of a tree and another two minutes to dig it up, pull it from its waterproof bag, and set it up. It was the Heckler and Koch 416 with RPG launcher attached. There was a bag of ten magazines and a grenade belt, which I hung around my shoulders. I took three seconds to steady my breathing and ran to the edge of the trees. There I detonated the first mine. It was damn loud in the silence of the night. A moment after detonation, the column collapsed and took with it the power line, killing the spotlights on the fence.

I detonated two more in rapid succession and ran for the fence. There I pulled a set of pliers from the rucksack, set about cutting through the fence, paused to detonate the fourth charge, and finished cutting myself a hole I could slip through. But I didn't slip through it. I waited thirty seconds because I had heard barking dogs and running boots. I scrambled back, pulling my Sig as I went. The dogs hurtled past, and the two handlers went after them. I scrambled through, cut a hole in the far fence, and ran like I had all the demons of hell on my tail toward the glow of the processing plant.

Ahead of me, maybe a quarter of a mile away, I could see five Land Rovers and four or five Jeeps race, bouncing and jerking over the rough ground, headed for the smoldering remains of the fence.

I figured I could ignore them for a minute and try and spot a place by the plant where I could hide. A hundred or a hundred and fifty yards away, I could see what I assumed to be the kilns where the lithium was dried. They reached temperatures close to two thousand degrees. As I approached the floodlit area, I began to see the children. Mostly they were around the mill pulling carts and dumping raw material into the funnels. Others were loading the carts from where the trucks dumped what they brought from the mining areas. But they were everywhere, doing every kind of menial unskilled job.

There were men and women too, and among them and around them, men with guns. But now the men with guns, instead of watching the workers, were staring away in the direction of the explosions.

I dropped beside the nearest kiln, pulled out my binoculars, and looked in the same direction as the guards. By the light of their headlights, I could see the Land Rovers and the Jeeps pulling up along the smoldering wreckage. Men started to climb down and inspect the damage. It was hard to be sure, but I made it between twenty and thirty men, some inspecting the damage, others taking up positions, pointing their weapons out into the dark. I pulled my cell and detonated the mines. There were four violent detonations in rapid succession, and eight thousand red-hot ball bearings ripped into the men covering an area of little more than thirty feet. When I checked with the binoculars again, I didn't see anybody standing.

I pulled my last four pounds of C4 from the rucksack, placed it under the belly of the kiln, and set the detonator. When I looked up, I could see the guards moving in confusion. The kids were crying and backing away toward what looked like sleeping quarters. Some of the guards seemed to be shouting at them to continue working, but others seemed to be panicking and shouting at each other.

I saw one of the guards grab a kid by the hair. The kid was so skinny and disheveled it was impossible to tell if it was a boy or a girl. The kid was screaming and struggling to get away. Another kid came running up and started hitting and kicking the guard. I tried to take aim, but the risk of hitting the kids was too high.

Then everything happened in a fraction of a second. He let go of the kid's hair and lashed out at both of them with his foot. They scrambled, and he put his rifle to his shoulder. I fired first and put a round through his head.

He went down rigid, like a wooden post. As he hit the dust, the other guards scrambled for a tall wooden structure that looked like the offices and administrative building. There was a cold rage in my belly. I figured at a rough estimate they were probably a hundred and twenty or a hundred and fifty feet away. I let them have two RPGs, and just before they hit their mark, I gave them a few bursts of automatic fire. A couple fell. Most made cover. In the distance, I could see a stream of trucks' headlights heading for the road.

Then the grenades exploded, and I ran.

I ran for where the conveyor belt entered the back end of the kiln. There I dropped and scrambled under the belt to the far side. There, there was a large esplanade where the processing plant made a kind of horse shoe. Right then, it was full of scattering, screaming kids and adults who were running for cover. It was the worst possible place they could be, but there was nothing I could do about that right then.

I crouched and ran along the conveyor, keeping low, headed toward the building that looked like the offices and administration. That was where most of the guards had piled in. When I was thirty yards away, I dropped on my belly, looking under the conveyor belt at the door, which stood open. I could see two guys in there peering out. They had rifles and were keeping watch.

That meant one of two things. They were contacting a superior, maybe Nelson, for instructions, or they were arranging some form of escape. That meant I had to act fast. Up to this point, they believed they were under attack, probably from government special forces. In another sixty seconds, they would start to realize they were under attack by one man. I had to keep the chaos going, and fast. Two more RPGs seemed like a good way to start.

I gave them two bursts of automatic fire and then let them

have two grenades through the open door. I waited for the first blast and ran for the corner of the building. I flattened myself against the wall and took a second to psych myself to burst through the door. That was when a screaming, hysterical kid of no more than ten collided with me from behind. He looked up into my face with wild eyes, opened his mouth, and screamed. I grabbed him and put my hand over his mouth.

"Escucha!" I said, which meant listen. "Escucha a mi!" H e stopped screaming. I pointed to myself. "Yo amigo. Tu." I pointed at him and then all around us. "Tu, familia, amigos," then I pointed down toward the fence I had destroyed. "Escapar! Go! Land Rover! Tu, amigos, familia, escapar!"

My meaning began to dawn on him, and he nodded like crazy, then turned and ran across the esplanade, screaming in Spanish, right across the line of fire from the office building. There was no time to psych myself. I went round the corner screaming like a Viking berserker, putting two grenades through the door and another through the window. In the seconds that followed, two guys came bundling out of the door, and I put three rounds into each of them. Then the door and the windows shattered.

I reloaded, kicked what was left of the door aside, and poked the HK through the smoldering opening. It was hard to tell the bits of burned wood and furniture from the scorched limbs. The place had been some kind of office. Now it was the antechamber to hell. I moved through it to a second, shattered, smoldering door in back.

There I found a bathroom and a stairwell, and I heard a rustle upstairs. I waited, motionless and silent. A rustle, a whisper. So there were at least two of them. I flattened my back against the wall with the 416 pointing up the stairs at the landing above. I moved sideways, like a crab, keeping the cannon trained on where they would appear. There was a heavy, oppressive silence and the choking smell of scorched flesh.

I arrived at the switchback and was now looking up the stairs at the landing. There was a dark corridor to the right and another to the left, dark tunnels that led to death—mine or theirs.

I put the rifle to my shoulder and took aim. I was going to lob a grenade down the corridor on my right, then charge down the passage on my left. I never got to pull the trigger. There was a roar and a scream that came out of the depths of fear and rage. I just had time to switch my finger to the assault rifle trigger. A huge, bloodstained, raging animal surged out of the passage. His hair and his beard were singed, his face was gashed, and his pants were soaked with blood. He was dying, but he was going down fighting.

Or that was what he thought. I put four rounds in his chest, and he fell in a heap at my feet. I waited a moment, looking at the guy on the floor. He must have been six three, with blond hair, and the dead eyes that were staring up at me were blue. Argentines are a mix; there are Scots, Irish, and Germans as well as Spanish and Indian. But the fact is most Argentines you meet are dark. Two got you twenty this guy was a mercenary, like half the guards at the mine.

I called out, "You speak English?"

There was a short pause, then a South African voice. "I'm hurt, pretty bad."

"Be smart, pal. Come on out, and we'll get you to the States for treatment. We got plenty of footage, but we need a witness to testify. Right now you're in a position to make a deal. Make us come up there and all deals are off."

"Okay, don't shoot. I'm coming out, and I'm unarmed."

"Nice and slow. How many of you are there?"

"Just me."

He shuffled around the corner. He had desert fatigues on and his hands up in the air. He was stained with blood like his pal. He looked rough. I indicated the steps.

"Sit down. You hurt bad? Do you need first aid?"

"I dunno. Maybe." He sat.

"Who runs this place?"

"Some corporation. We're an independent contractor out of New York. I'm just a grunt, mate."

"Day to day."

"Mr. McCormack, he runs things on a day-to-day basis. Mate, I'm pretty bad. I don't know if I can hold out much longer."

I nodded like I understood. "Sure. I'll call the guys. The Aquanecra Security Corporation? You were in Iraq and Afghanistan, right?"

"Yeah." He was shaking and sweating profusely. "I really need a doctor, mate."

I shook my head. "No you don't. You abuse and enslave children, you don't need a doctor. With me around, mate, what you need is an undertaker."

I put a round through his forehead. With any luck, his dying thought was that it wasn't smart to use kids as slaves.

I took his car keys from his pocket, then checked the top floor. I didn't find anybody. I wondered briefly if there would have been more people during the day. I figured there would have, but I guess you have to draw the line somewhere.

Looking out the window, I saw small clusters of kids, men and women, running, scattering into the night.

I went down and stepped out into the empty plant.

SIXTEEN

AT THE BACK OF THE ADMINISTRATION BUILDING, there was a parking lot. A section of it was reserved for cars and small trucks, like Land Rovers and Jeeps. The farther section was for the big trucks that brought the raw material for the processing plant. Adjacent to that part of the lot was a mechanics' garage where they carried out the maintenance on the trucks. In there, I found what I expected: gas pumps for diesel and gasoline to fuel the trucks, big and small, and the administrative staff's cars.

It took me forty-five minutes, but I doused the office building in enough gas to burn Rome, then I opened and overturned the steel drums until the whole damn place was awash with octane.

When I was done, I took the South African guy's fob from my pocket and pressed the open button. A Jeep at the far end of the lot flashed and bleeped. In my pocket, I had a disposable lighter I had brought along for the purpose. I ignited the gasoline on the blacktop and watched the blue flames dance through the darkness into the cavern of the garage. Then I turned and walked toward the Jeep.

As I climbed behind the wheel, I could see the flames surging violently inside the building. Soon the temperatures would soar and the diesel in the tanks would erupt. Already the flames were licking into the wooden administrative building. I started the engine and drove north toward the gate. When I was half a mile from the plant, I stopped and pulled my cell from my pocket. I pressed nine, and there was the almost instantaneous report of a detonation.

Then the sky lit up. A blast of hot air rocked the Jeep, and the kiln erupted in a massive explosion of intense heat and ignited gasses. I shielded my eyes and watched a sheet of flame engulf the processing plant. I floored the pedal and made off along the drive toward the gate.

It was a two-mile drive along a straight road, and I covered it in a little over one minute. As I approached, the gate stood open. There I slowed and skidded to a halt to look back. The glow was intense, more intense than it had been with the spotlights. The brigadier's friends would be happy. They'd pick up their mine for a song now.

I pulled out of the gate and headed toward Poman.

It was just after nine p.m. when I got there. The iron gates to Rosario's house were closed, but I could see a faint glow in a couple of the windows. So I pulled up to the gate, did a U-turn so my trunk was six feet away, put the vehicle in reverse, and floored the pedal. There was a moment while the tires skidded in the dirt, then they gripped and hurled the truck backward. The gate sprang open, wobbled, and lurched to the side. I spun the wheel, put it in drive, and pulled up outside the door.

I swung down from the cab with the Sig in my hand. I put a round through the lock on the door and kicked it open. Nothing happened. There was no volley of shots, no screaming, no shouting. The door swung in, hit the wall, and swung slowly back a few inches.

I stepped in, saw the spacious living room with its open fireplace and the plate glass sliding doors out to the patio. I waited and listened. There was nothing at first, then the murmur of voices in conversation. It made me frown. A semi-automatic taking out a lock in a quiet village in the Andes makes a noise. It makes the kind of noise that would stop a conversation over dinner.

Besides that, what the hell were they doing having a conversation over dinner? Had they not been informed that the mine had just been destroyed?

I stepped inside. Absently I noted the sound of two cars outside. I moved across the drawing room, passed the cold fireplace, and stopped at the plate glass doors, which stood open.

They were at a table that had been set with a white linen tablecloth, crystal glasses, and two decanters of wine. There was food on the table, roast meat, dishes of potatoes and vegetables. Seated at the head was the senator, Kit O'Hanlon. On his right was Mat Coren and on his left Nigel Hunt. They watched me while they chewed. The senator leaned back in his seat and sipped his wine. He spoke as he set down his glass.

"So you did your worst, Harry. Yet here we still are."

"I am not done yet, Senator. And here you still are, but my guess is you're hurting. Where's Angela?"

He reached for his knife and fork and spoke without looking at me. "That's Lady Angela to you, and where she is is none of your damned business. She's not here, and pretty soon neither will you be."

I was aware that the two cars had pulled up outside the house and stopped. Now I was aware of a presence behind me. At least two men, probably more. I figured I had one or two seconds before I was shot in the back and stepped out into the patio and moved toward their table, watching their faces. Anyone shooting me now would risk hitting one of these billionaire clowns. Their eyes were flicking like hooked fish between me and whoever was behind me. I smiled as I moved around the table and stood behind O'Hanlon, with a hand on each shoulder, looking back at the glass doors.

There was Nelson, the mayor, with a police sergeant and three local tough guys. I jerked my chin at the cop. "You speak English?"

He shook his head. I looked at the three guys in turn. They were in their thirties, swarthy, probably part Indian. One of them had long hair in a ponytail. The guy by his side had a big mustache. The third guy was better dressed than the other two, and his hair was groomed. I asked him the same question. "You? You speak English?"

He also shook his head. So I wracked my brain for some basic Spanish. "Tiene hijos?" Did they have children?

They weren't the most expressive guys in the world, but I saw their brows contract an eighth of an inch. However lightly, I had touched a nerve. The cop snapped, "Basta!" and pulled his gun.

Without rushing or making sudden movement, I reached down and pulled the Fairbairn and Sykes from my boot and placed the tip against the side of O'Hanlon's neck. I felt him go rigid.

I looked at the guy with the ponytail. "Donde esta su hijos?"

I knew the grammar was a mess, but I was doing the best I could, asking him where his kids were. He turned and looked at the mayor. The mayor ignored him and shouted at the sergeant, "Mátelo ya!" which I figured was like, kill him already.

I took a fistful of O'Hanlon's hair in my left hand and pricked his skin with the tip of the knife. He shuddered, went rigid, and shouted, "No! Wait! Wait!"

The sergeant began to speak, but I interrupted him and repeated, "Donde esta su hijos?" Everyone was getting real nervous. I looked at the guy with the moustache. "Tu hijo esclavo en mina." His kid was a slave at the mine. I thought a moment. "Ahora libre."

Now he was free.

The mayor started shouting, first at his tough guys, then at the sergeant, thrusting his finger at me. The hired muscle was looking real unhappy. I kept my eyes fixed on them and jerked my head toward the door. "Go!" I said. "Go and look! Hijos esclavos libre! Mira!" I jerked my chin at the door again. "Mira!"

They were looking. They were looking every which way. They

were looking at each other, at the door, and at the mayor. And that made the mayor make a big mistake. He pointed hysterically at the guy with the moustache and screamed at the cop, "Mátelo!" *Kill him.*

A bigger mistake was when the sergeant switched his gun from me to the guy with the moustache. I didn't hesitate. I drove the knife up to the hilt into O'Hanlon's neck, and in one fluid movement, while they were screaming at each other, I pulled the Sig from under my arm and put a 9mm slug through the sergeant's head. Next thing, the mayor was backing away, holding out both hands in front of him like he could stop a bullet with them. O'Hanlon was gurgling in his chair with blood oozing over the blade on both sides of his neck. I pulled the trigger and blew out Nelson McCormack's left knee. He screamed like a woman and fell writhing on the floor.

I put the Sig back under my arm, took hold of the hilt of the knife, and punched forward. The senator died in less than a second. Nigel and Mat were trembling badly. They had gone the color of candle wax with hepatitis.

I pointed at the door with the bloody knife. "Yo destruir mina. Hijos, hombres, mujeres..." I struggled to think of the word and flicked my hands in a 'go away' gesture. "Ir," I said. "Esclavos ir." I had told them as best I could that I had destroyed the mine and the slaves had gone. Now I pointed at them. "Go, go get your kids. Ir! Ir a tus hijos!"

The guy with the ponytail looked down at the sobbing mayor. I couldn't make out the words, but I got that he was asking him if it was true. The mayor looked at them all, his bottom lip curling in under his teeth. All I caught was "Perdón, perdón," and "Ayuda..."

He was asking for forgiveness and help, the compassion and the empathy he had been incapable of showing the children of his own village. The Indian pulled a knife from his belt, knelt beside the mayor, who was screaming, "No! No! Por Dios! No!" and cut through his throat.

There was a lot of blood. The man stood and looked at me. He said, "Gracias," and they left. I put the knife in its sheath and pulled the Sig.

Nigel was saying, "Now look, we didn't know -"

"Try and run and I will shoot you dead."

I said that as I moved behind Mat and pulled his chair back at a forty-five degree angle. As I did it, I shot him in the right knee. He screamed, clutching his leg and repeating, "Oh God! Oh God!"

"You're looking for compassion now, Mat?" I didn't wait for an answer. I looked across the table at Nigel. "I'm going to ask you once. Then I am going to blow off your knee. Where is Angela?"

He held up both hands, waving them in the negative. "No! No, listen, we don't know -"

I was halfway around the table. He scrambled to his feet, whimpering, and turned to run. I shot him through the back of his right knee. He fell on his face, sobbing and crying out, "Ow! Ow!"

I spoke quietly. "You're crying like a child. But you know something? The kids I saw at the mine, skinny, barefoot and bruised, they weren't crying. Their pain and their suffering had taken them beyond crying."

I turned back to Mat. "Now it's the other knee. Where is Angela?"

He held my eye. Tears were streaming down his face. His lips were trembling. I counted three in my mind and shot out his other knee. He threw back his head and made a grotesque, inhuman noise. I felt sick. Everything inside me wanted to feel pity and compassion. But all I could think of was those bastards with assault rifles and the starving, terrified kids ripped from their homes and abused.

And if Angela lived, she would do it again.

I walked over to Nigel, lying face down in a pool of his own blood.

"For God's sake, Harry, listen to me."

"I'm listening."

"You don't understand the repercussions."

"The repercussions are irrelevant to you, Nigel. Either you tell me and I get you to a hospital, or you don't and I keep blowing bits off you till you bleed out and die."

"You don't know who she is. You don't realize who she is."

"The money she's investing, it's Chinese?" He was nodding. "You have three seconds to tell me where she is. After that, I am going to start cutting bits off you with my knife."

"No, no, please stop! I'll tell you. But please, for God's sake, we need protection."

"You've got it. She won't hurt you."

"Los Angeles. She has a house in Beverly Hills." He gave me a number on Bedford Drive. "She's gone back there for meetings with her Chinese contacts and..." He hesitated. I said, "And who?"

"Carol Hennessy, of the Hennessy Foundation. They hold a major stake in the mine. There will be hell to pay for what you've done."

I was quiet for a moment. Then, "For what I have done?"

I put a single slug through the back of his head. Then I turned and walked back to look across the table at Mat. He was still sobbing. "You said if we talked..."

"I said if you talked she wouldn't hurt you. She won't hurt you because you, like her, will be dead. It's like an algorithm, Mat."

I shot him through the head.

I stepped out into the night. I climbed into the truck, opened the windows, and pulled out through the shattered gate. If I'd had the choice, I would have walked, but time was a consideration, and I wanted to be in Catamarca by dawn. But I drove slowly, letting the cool air hit my face.

It took me less than two minutes to reach the hotel. I killed the engine and left the truck outside. I pushed through the door and hammered the bell on the reception desk. Carla appeared from the breakfast room after a couple of seconds and froze. She stood staring at me.

"What have you done?"

"The mine is destroyed. The kids are free. There were men and women there too, from the villages. They took the Land Rovers and the Jeeps and ran. You should go and look for your daughter, Lucia."

She put her hands to her mouth. Tears sprang from her eyes. She came toward me, reaching for my face. "Gracias, gracias, dios mío!"

She clung to me and squeezed, repeating her thanks over and over. I took her shoulders and pushed her gently away. "The mayor is dead, the chief of police also, and most of the owners of the mine. The guards are all dead. Take the car outside, call the mothers and the fathers, organize a search. Many will have returned to the villages, Colana, Mutquín, Mischango, but if you take flashlights to the mine, spread out, call them, get organized..."

I trailed off, feeling suddenly exhausted, gutted, empty inside. She nodded, kissed my face more times than was necessary, and ran out to the truck, shouting women's names. Her neighbors, I figured.

I thought about getting my own truck and heading down to Catamarca. Instead I found my feet taking me to the kitchen in search of whiskey.

I poured myself a large measure, pulled off half, then took my phone and called the brigadier. He answered on the first ring.

"Harry."

"It's done. Almost."

"Almost?"

I rubbed my eyes with my fingers and took another pull on the whiskey. "I feel sick."

"Are you all right?"

"No," I said with more spite than he deserved. "I feel sick. The processing plant is destroyed. I blew the kiln. The kids and the

Indians escaped. Carla's getting a search party together to look for the kids."

"You said almost."

"Yeah, I'm getting there. I killed all the guards. Then I came into town and I killed Senator Kit O'Hanlon, Nigel Hunt, Mat Coren, the mayor of the town, Nelson McCormack, and the chief of police. I don't know what his name was."

"Harry, are you all right? I am serious, you sound as though you're in trouble."

"No, I am not all right. I feel sick. It's too much killing for one day. But I'm having a whiskey. I'll be okay in a while." Thee was a moment's silence, and I said, "But Lady Angela Liu got away. She went to Los Angeles. She has a house in Beverly Hills, on Bedford Drive. She has meetings arranged with her Chinese masters." I paused, then added, "And Carol Hennessy of the Hennessy Foundation. The foundation holds a major stake in the mine."

"Stay where you are, Harry. I'm going to send someone to get you. Are you at your hotel in Poman?"

"Yeah."

"Go to your room. Try to get some sleep. I'll have someone there within the hour."

I held the phone in front of me and frowned at it. Nothing made much sense. I could hear his voice real far away, saying my name. "Harry? Can you hear me?"

I nodded. "Yeah," I said quietly. "I can hear you. Come and get me. You better come too. I might kill whoever it is if I don't know their face..."

I hung up and went up to my room.

SEVENTEEN

I HAVE NO CLEAR RECOLLECTION OF THEIR ARRIVAL. I know I heard the chopper. I remember the brigadier hunkered down beside me, peering into my face, and some wiseass saying, "He's drunk the whole bottle..."

Then I remember the whole world tilting and swimming and falling away beneath me and flying. And I remember a soft lap and a soft hand stroking my face and reassuring myself it could not be the brigadier. Because he didn't wear a blue skirt, and his hands were like concrete.

Then darkness.

It was a darkness that was timeless. It seemed to go on into infinity, like the darkness of space. Sometimes I would awaken, or believe I was awake, and just see the vast, incalculable void, the empty blackness of my existence. Sometimes there were people talking to me, saying things like, "Well, you emptied your life." And there was a woman who told me, "You used up all your credit, you emptied the account."

I knew I was flying. Because a couple of times I opened my eyes and I could see the row of translucent portholes, and once I saw the moonlight on the wing.

When I opened my eyes again, I was in a bed. The curtains

were open, and so was the window, and there was early sunlight. There were birds singing small, sporadic songs, and a very soft breeze occasionally moved the curtain. Through the window, I could see the leaves of a sycamore and a solitary cloud in a blue sky. My mind was silent. All the soft sounds were on the outside, but on the inside, there was just silence and peace.

I don't know how long I lay like that, maybe five minutes, maybe half an hour, but eventually, I heard a noise that was inside the room. I turned my head, feeling the cool linen on my face, and frowned. The colonel, Colonel Jane Harrison, was curled in a large armchair beside the bed. She was in a blue skirt and white blouse. On her lap, she had an open book face down, and her eyes were closed.

I smiled. It hadn't been the brigadier's blue skirt and soft hands, then. I lay like that for another long while, watching her sleeping. When she eventually opened her eyes, I smiled at her. She didn't return the smile. She rubbed her face and ran her fingers through her hair.

"Fell asleep," she said. Then, "How are you feeling?"

"Peaceful, like somebody doped me. Can you smile?"

She gave it a try and failed. "Ever, or just right now?" The question was too complicated for me, so I ignored it. She said, "Right now it's kind of difficult. We were worried about you."

"I'm okay. I'll be fine once I've rested. It would help if you smiled."

"I'm working on it, Harry. You want some breakfast?"

I nodded. "Coffee and croissants." She stood. I asked her, "Are you going to stay?"

Now she smiled, but it was a sad smile. "Yes, I'm going to stay."

She stepped out the door, and I slipped back into the blackness.

I eventually joined them on the second floor terrace of one of the few houses on Ocean Avenue, opposite Palisades Park. It was five-thirty in the late afternoon, and the sun was hovering over the vast blue shoot of the Pacific, casting a crazy path of sparkling photons all the way to hell.

The colonel had a long, ice-cold gin and tonic in her hand. The brigadier had a Macallan, and there was a guy in a white jacket and white gloves hovering over me. I told him, "Bushmills, straight up."

The brigadier added, "The twenty-one-year-old," and the guy in the gloves disappeared. The colonel and the brigadier watched me pull out a chair and sit. He put words to the expression on her face.

"How are you feeling?"

I thought about it and shook my head. "How long have I been unconscious? Even if you had a Gulfstream parked in the back yard, that's at least eighteen hours."

The colonel said, "Thirty-six, but we sedated you when we found you in your room. You were not well."

I grunted. "So Angela has been gone maybe forty-eight hours."

"She's at home, in Beverly Hills. We are keeping tabs on her."

"What's her security like?"

It was the colonel who answered. "It's everything you would expect. Her personal bodyguards are Jo Luomo, ex Delta Force, Nick McKenna, also Delta, Alex Kent from the Special Boat Service, and Bob de Vries, Navy Seal. As well as those guys, she has a permanent guard on the house made up of a dozen experienced mercenaries from the Aquanecra Security Corporation. There are cameras, dogs, and everything else a paranoid billionaire might decide she needs." She paused and drew breath, looking at her glass. "But Harry..."

I heard everything I needed to hear in the tone of her voice. I shook my head. "No, don't go there."

It was the brigadier who answered. "Just listen to her, Harry."

Most of the time I do what the brigadier says. So I shut my mouth and tried not to look hostile.

She said again, "Harry, you're not well."

"What the hell is that supposed to mean?"

"If you'll shut up for just five minutes, I might get the chance to tell you."

I took a deep breath and nodded once. The guy with the white gloves appeared carrying a silver tray and placed a glass of Bushmills in front of me. I thanked him. He went away, and I sipped, watching the colonel over the edge of my glass.

"You have been saying for a long time that you want to stop working. What you did in Poman—" She shook her head. "I know the best of the best, and I don't know anyone who could have pulled off what you did." She caught the look on my face and arched an eyebrow. "Believe me, Harry, I am not flattering you. In the first place, I don't waste my time on people who need flattery, and in the second place, I wouldn't waste my time trying to flatter you."

I frowned, not sure whether I had just been flattered twice or not. I said, "All that aside, Angela got away."

"Try not to talk, Harry." It was the brigadier. "Just listen and think about what Jane is telling you."

"It's a miracle you got out alive, Harry. You not only did that, but you dealt them a very severe blow too."

"Why do I feel there is a but coming?"

"Because when we found you, you were a wreck. I'm giving it to you straight, Harry, the good and the bad. I don't know anyone who could have done what you did, let alone come out alive. But you are hurt – more than that, you are damaged. No less than if you'd taken a couple of rounds to the chest."

"Bullshit."

I said it without much conviction. She made a *really?* face and asked me, "You want me to give you the details?"

I glanced at the brigadier. All he did was raise his eyebrows. I said, "Sure, give me the details."

"You were weeping."

"They were shooting at children with automatic weapons."

"You were *begging* to stop killing, Harry."

"Come on!" I looked at the brigadier, and he nodded.

"You had lost count of the people you had killed, and you were saying you had lost your humanity and your compassion."

"Both are overrated."

"You don't believe that, and if you do, then you have no place in Cobra. You know damn well, Harry, that Cobra is all about humanity and compassion."

"Okay, okay, so what's your point, Colonel?"

"Will you please call me Jane?"

"Jane, what is your point?"

"I want you to stop."

"*What?*"

"I want you to stop working. You have told us many times you want to stop, and we have pestered you into going back. We were wrong, and we have done you a lot of harm. I have discussed it with the brigadier, and we want you to retire."

I frowned and shook my head. What she was saying was true. I had been trying to retire for a long time, but the brigadier had always found a way to pull me back. Perhaps more to the point, I had always known that he would try to pull me back. Now he and Jane, and Cobra itself, were telling me I was no longer fit for the job.

The brigadier seemed to read my mind.

"I know what you're thinking, Harry. But in a sense, it's the contrary. If your action is anything to go by, you are becoming more efficient, better at what you do, but Jane and I are, above and beyond anything else, your friends, and what we are asking ourselves is, at what cost? As you get better at the job, what is the job doing to you? We were both shaken and deeply distressed by the way we found you, Harry. I agree with Jane, it is time to call it a day and seek some kind of healing."

"Healing?" There was more bitterness in my tone than I had intended. "What's next, we start greeting each other with 'Namaste'?"

The brigadier surprised me by laughing. "No, Harry. But you

and I both know, because we have discussed it on more than one occasion, that there comes a point when a warrior stops killing. That happens either because he gets killed or because he changes his path and takes up Zen Buddhism or some form of meditation." He gave his head a small shake. "You have killed a lot of people, Harry, and whether you are aware of it or not, something inside you needs to process what you have done and give it some kind of meaning."

I took a pull on the whiskey, smacked my lips, and as I set down the glass, I said, "I'll tell you what I am going to do. I am not even going to think about what you're telling me"—I paused —"until after I have killed Angela. When Angela is dead and those children are avenged, I will go to the Wind River Mountains, to Sacred Rim, and I will think about everything you have said to me. But not before I have looked Angela in the eye and paid her for what she did to those children."

Jane closed her eyes and drew breath, but the brigadier silenced her. He said, "Agreed. But the moment the job is done, you retire."

I nodded a few times, staring at my whiskey. "The moment the job is done, I will think about what you're telling me." I looked up at the brigadier. "I'll go to the winds, and I'll think about it."

There was bitterness and anger in the colonel's voice when she said, "You want to share that with me, or is this just for the guys?"

I turned and looked her in the eye. I remembered her asleep in the chair beside my bed. I remembered my head in her lap on the plane. I smiled. It wasn't a happy smile. It was more an apologetic one.

"I'm sorry. It is not just for the guys. Once the job is finished, I will go up in the Winds, to Sacred Rim, and I will think about what you are telling me. But not before."

She sat forward and pointed at me. "I can see I am outvoted here, but I will not agree to this without making something very clear. If you go after Angela Liu in the emotional, mental state you are in, you may well get yourself killed. But if you don't, if you pull this off, the damage it does to you, mentally and emotionally, may be irreversible."

I nodded, leaving traces of the smile on my face. "I know," I said, "but I am afraid that ship has already sailed. I take out Angela Liu. Then we'll see what happens next."

She looked at the brigadier. There was bright anger in her eyes. He didn't say anything. She stood.

"If you'll excuse me, I don't think there is any more I can add to this discussion."

She moved around the table, and as she reached the sliding glass doors, I said, "Jane."

She turned back. Her cheeks were flushed with anger. I said, "Thanks. When this is over, can we talk?"

She turned and left. We heard the door. I didn't exactly smile, but only because I was fighting hard not to.

The brigadier studied me a moment and sighed. "You know I agree with her."

"I would too, if I was in your shoes."

"Frankly, I think you are doing yourself a lot of harm with this crusade. You are pushing yourself well beyond your limits, and it's telling on you."

"But?"

"But knowing you as I do, I think if you didn't finish the job, it would cause you more anxiety still."

"You are right. I can't betray those kids."

"Or the little girl in Helmand. But at some point, you have to come to terms with two facts, Harry. First, you are not responsible for that little girl in Helmand, or any of the other children in the world who are being abused and exploited. And second, you cannot save them all, however hard you try."

I was quiet for a long time, looking out at the ocean. I saw the sun settle on the still water and bleed fire into the sea and the sky. A cool breeze touched my face.

"If I am not responsible, if you are not responsible, and all of these millions and billions of people are not responsible, then who is? The guys who perpetrate these crimes? So if those guys are the only ones responsible, you tell me, how do we solve this? Because they don't give a damn, and they are going to go right on doing it."

It was maybe ten or fifteen minutes later that he said, "I am not sure how to answer that, Harry. Maybe that's why I am letting you finish the job."

EIGHTEEN

I WAS IN A RANGE ROVER BECAUSE IF YOU DON'T WANT to attract unwelcome attention on Bedford Avenue, in Beverly Hills, you have to drive a vehicle whose price would buy you a house in any other neighborhood. I was on the corner of Carmelita and Bedford watching her house a hundred yards away. It was eight in the morning, and I had been there half an hour already. So far, I had seen no activity.

Ten minutes later, I saw a Rolls Royce Black Badge roll out of the drive. It cruised past me and headed east toward Santa Monica Boulevard. I gave it two minutes, figuring it should not be too hard to follow, did a U-turn, and went after it.

They followed the boulevard at a steady pace, and I allowed myself to fall back, leaving several cars behind us. We came eventually to Hollywood, where they slowed and turned north into Vine Street. I followed them north as far as Sunset Boulevard, where they turned left and pulled into the parking garage beneath the tower block on the corner of Argyle Avenue.

I drove on by on Argyle for two hundred yards and parked across from the Camden. Then I climbed out and walked back to the corner of Sunset Boulevard. The Cobra Intelligence Department had told us Angela Liu was on the board of directors of the

Ai Corporation, whose motto was Love and Affection, which was apparently what Ai meant in Chinese. The Ai Love and Affection Corporation was a Chinese company but had its American head office in the two top floors of that tower of steel and glass.

I had no particular plan. My instinct was just to walk in and shoot her and to hell with the consequences, but I knew that was not realistically possible. Her security would be at a maximum right then, and even God would have to be scanned and strip-searched before he got to see her.

I climbed the stairs and entered the lobby. The guy in the blue uniform on security ignored me, and I moved across the green marble floor to the elevators. Beside them was a list of all the companies with offices there. The Ai Love and Affection Corporation occupied the 21st and 22nd floors, right at the top.

There were half a dozen people waiting. One of the elevators pinged, and on an impulse, I followed the crowd in. There were only twenty buttons on the pad beside the door. There was a guy in a suit standing beside me. I smiled at him and pointed to the buttons.

"What do I do if I want to go to the 22nd floor?"

He chuckled. "You get the Love and Affection Corporation to issue you with a chip in a key-card." He pointed. "There's a sensor just above number twenty. But I doubt you'll get one. That's highly classified stuff they do up there." Then he tinged his smile with a frown. "You're not a journalist, are you?"

I laughed. "That obvious, huh? Investigative reporter."

The elevator stopped. He said, "Good luck" and left with most of the crowd.

I got out on the twentieth floor and snooped around like I was looking for an office that I couldn't find. Nobody seemed to notice me, so I pushed into the service stairwell and climbed half a flight, to where it made the switchback. There I found myself looking up at a steel door with a large red sign pasted to it. The sign said, *Ai Security Systems, no admittance beyond this point.*

I took the first step, intending to examine the lock, and a female version of an electronic voice spoke.

"You are trespassing on Ai Property. Please turn around and leave. Security will be alerted in ten, nine, eight."

It stopped when I returned to the landing. I returned to the twentieth floor and took the elevator back down, then strolled back to the truck with my hands in my pockets, watching my feet and trying to unravel the Chinese puzzle in my head. At the mine, security had not been an issue because they never saw me coming, and their whole purpose was to keep people in, not out. But here, Angela knew I was coming for her, and she was using the most advanced technology available to keep me out.

And one thought I told myself I should be considering was once she had made her defensive move, what came next? Was she going to start gunning for me?

I climbed behind the wheel, slammed the door, and spent a while drumming my fingers on the steering wheel. My phone rang. It was the brigadier.

"Harry, where are you?"

"Argyle." I heard him draw breath but interrupted him. "I need a couple of drones, sir. And we need to talk."

"Agreed. Something has come up which you need to consider."

"I'm on my way."

"Meet me at the Blue Water Grill on Redondo Beach, Harry."

It was a forty-five minute drive. I left the Range Rover in the parking lot beside a burgundy S-Type Jaguar which I just knew was his and walked inside. I found him sitting beside a plate glass window with views of the marina. He had a dish of oysters in front of him, and he was sipping a glass of chilled fino.

I sat opposite him.

"People tend to drink champagne or Guinness with oysters. I find champagne too light and Guinness too strong. A Manzanilla fino, or a Moriles, is the perfect accompaniment. How was your morning?"

"My morning was instructive. It would be easier to raid Fort Knox and get away with all the gold there than it would be to get close enough to say good morning to Angie."

"Agreed."

"So I need two drones and a two-man team..."

I trailed off, studying his face. It hadn't changed in any way, but there was something about the steady stare he was giving me. I said, "What?"

"A development you may want to consider before you go any further."

If anyone else had said that to me, I would have told them to go to hell, but I knew if he was saying that, he had good reason. He was about the only person on the planet who knew me, and we shared a very similar view of life.

"Rosario contacted me last night."

I sagged back in my chair. The waiter came up. I bit back the impulse to tell him to go to hell and ordered a steak and an amber ale. When he'd gone, I said, "I don't understand. You didn't pick her up in Argentina? Isn't she with her father?"

"Yes to both. We have our own witness protection scheme, Harry, for very high-risk informants. She is safe in Altadena, at the foot of the mountains. It's a nice place. In some cases, we give them a contact number, where cases are ongoing or there is a serious risk. It seems she tried to contact me personally on a couple of occasions while I was still in Argentina. She contacted me again last night."

"What about? Why are you telling me this?"

"She wanted to know if you were all right, and she wanted to talk to you."

I closed my eyes and shook my head. "I don't need this, sir."

"Are you sure? It's something only you can know, but as an outside observer who knows you quite well, I would say maybe this is exactly what you need."

"What I need, sir, is to focus."

He nodded and slipped an oyster in his mouth. "On what?

All those years ago, when you first came to us after you captured Mohammed Ben-Amini, and I gave you the option of resigning the regiment, you were intensely focused on one thing. Do you remember?"[1]

"I was focused on Ben-Amini back then, the Butcher of Al-Landy."

"For a very similar reason. You watched him massacre an entire village, but it was the children that really got to you."

"What's your point, sir?"

"You have done a lot of jobs for Cobra; some have involved avenging children, some have involved rescuing children. I'll be honest with you, Harry: I knew for a certainty when I went to see you that you would take this job as soon as you knew there were kids involved. You are intensely focused on avenging one child whom you watched being abused and murdered in Al-Landy and you were not able to help or rescue."

My belly was on fire, and I could feel my heart pumping hard in my chest. I kept a tight rein on my voice and asked again, "Your point, sir."

"I'm getting there, Harry. I want you to listen and think about what I am saying. How many people have you killed? How many people have you killed seeking to avenge that girl? In Argentina alone in the last couple of weeks, it must have been dozens. The colonel told you, and I will back her up, she didn't know of one single operative who was capable of doing what you did that night." He raised one finger. "I attribute that to one thing: your focus, your concentrated attention. Your attention concentrated on one thing – retribution. Retribution for one girl whom you could not save back in Afghanistan." He leaned back in his chair. "I have one question for you. Has any of this retribution, have any of these killings, brought peace to you or this child?"

---

1. See *The Dead of Night*

I stared at him. There were no words in my head. There was just silence. The waiter brought my beer and set it in front of me.

The brigadier took a deep breath. "I am not given to feeling guilty, Harry. But in your case, I feel perhaps I have been insensitive to your needs. I have always considered you more of a friend than an operative, but perhaps as a friend, I have failed you." He tapped the table a few times with his middle finger. "Focus. Your capacity for focus is exceptional, but all these years, you have been focusing on retribution – let's speak plainly – on death." He gestured at me with his open hand. "It's a cliché, but it's true: You get more of what you focus on, and the focus you have – the rather intense focus you have - is killing you inside. Physically, you are practically indestructible, but what is happening to your soul, Harry?"

I drew breath to say something, but he raised his hand to stop me.

"In a rather long-winded way, I am making the point that perhaps it is time to focus on something else."

I frowned. "On what?"

He gave a short laugh. "It is perhaps a sad reflection on both of us that we have found it so hard to imagine the possibility of focusing on anything other than killing. But what if you focused on making a rather special woman happy? What if you used your extraordinary ability to focus on creating instead, on making a partnership with her?" He shrugged. "I hardly know the woman, but she is clearly intelligent, she is a lawyer, she has operated at an international level. You are by now a very rich man. What would happen, Harry, if you focused on each other, and on helping children? You already finance a foundation along those lines, don't you? Well, what if you both focused on that, as friends, as lovers, as a couple? Whatever you want to be, that's up to you. But it is an alternative focus for your mind, Harry – to create rather than destroy."

I picked up my beer and took a long pull. As I set down the glass, I said, "Talk about left field."

"I spoke to her for about half an hour. She had a lot to say about you, and practically all of it was complimentary. She seemed to think that she had not conveyed her gratitude to you and asked if you could meet. I told her I would talk to you." He hesitated a moment, then added, "I know you have feelings for her, Harry. Life may be giving you a second chance."

I puffed out my cheeks and blew. "I tried this once before and almost got Claire killed."[2]

"I know. Perhaps in the past, I was not as helpful as I could have been. You were a very valuable asset to us, and I wasn't keen to see you go. You still are a valuable asset." He shook his head. "But I can't stand by and watch you going through what you went through the other night."

"Help how?" I frowned at the table, then raised my eyes to look at him.

"We can make you disappear and become somebody else. We can kill you off and create a new past."

"I don't know sir. I need to finish this job."

"Do you? Are you sure? What would happen if you didn't? What would happen if you focused on something else?"

"I don't know..."

"Will you at least talk to her?"

He reached in his pocket and slid a card across the table. I stared at it a moment before picking it up. I looked at the number, then slipped it into my wallet.

"Okay, I'll call her. And I'll think about everything you have said. It is true I have been wanting to retire. Helping kids would be good." I took a deep breath. "Meantime, I need two drones, and I need a two-man team."

He smiled. "You, or whoever takes over from you if you do the smart thing."

"Yeah." I nodded. "Me or that guy."

---

2. See *Riding the Devil*

NINETEEN

We discussed over lunch how I would approach the hit on Angela. He listened with care while he ate a very tender sirloin with a few token asparagus tips, two slices of zucchini, and one slice of eggplant. At the more challenging parts, he would pause to sip his wine.

I finished by saying, "If we don't do it like that, I don't think it can be done."

He did something that started out as a sigh but turned into a grunt. "It's very ambitious. It would take a lot of preparation and string-pulling in a very short amount of time."

I knew he was talking to himself, so I focused on my sirloin and found he was right: You did get more of what you focused on. While I ate, he made a couple of phone calls.

"Put me through to props, will you?"

He stared at me, chewing his lip, while I chewed my steak and sipped my wine. Then he blinked and said, "Jim, look, I need a couple of drones. One small, small enough to fly under a car and release a magnetized RTD. I need it yesterday. Good, now for this next thing, I am going to rely on your genius. I need a very fast drone, several hundred miles per hour... No it doesn't need to go very far, no more than a mile or two – yes, exactly like a drag race,

Jim. But it needs to carry a payload of between fifty and a hundred pounds."

There was a protracted silence. After fifteen seconds, the brigadier said, "Jim?" Then, "No, no, don't explain to me how you are going to do it. You are far too intelligent, and I would never understand. The important thing is it can be done."

He took a deep breath and watched me a moment, blinking. Finally he said, "If you stay up all night, you can have it by nine in the morning. That will be fine. Thank you, Jim."

He put away his phone and leaned back in his chair.

"So how does this play out? You sit on her house, and when she emerges at eight in the morning, as she does every day, you send a very fast, very small drone under her Rolls and plant a remote tracking device under her car. Later in the day, when she has returned home, you send in the second drone, flying low. You come in at the rear of the house, over her back yard because you believe the building will be less reinforced here and deliver one hundred pounds of C4 against one of the back windows."

"It's not just that the back is less likely to be bulletproof and bombproof. There are also less likely to be collateral casualties."

"Right. And at this point, our team, drilling three or four roads away, cut the power supply to her house."

I nodded. "Ai is only as invincible as its power supply. The cameras go down, alarm systems go down, panic rooms open..." I shrugged.

"So her team bundle her out the front door to put her in the Rolls, and you take them as they get in the car."

"Right, but if that fails for any reason, too much movement, chaos, too many people – whatever - we can track the car and hit it on the way to wherever her fallback location is."

"You know that car is a tank."

I shrugged. "I know, but without any intelligence on where they will go, it's impossible to make a more detailed plan. For all we know, she might go to her office on Sunset Boulevard. Or she might head out to the mountains. If the hit fails at her door, all we can do is improvise."

He nodded a few times, staring out at the marina. Finally he said, "Then you need a more powerful weapon to make the hit."

"Okay." I echoed his nod. "I block the drive with the Range Rover and hit them with RPGs, then get out, confirm the kill, and go."

"If you decide not to do it, I'll put a team on it."

"Let me think about it. I'm not comfortable handing this over. It has to be done right. The RPGs have to ricochet off the wall behind them. The blast has to catch them between the Rolls and the house."

"I know." He waited a moment, then said, "Harry, go and phone Rosario. Whatever else happens, if you go ahead with this job, I don't want you thinking about a woman while you do it. Go and phone her and resolve this one way or another. You know my thoughts, but you must do what you think best." I went to stand, and he slid the keys to the Jaguar across the table. "Take the Jag. Leave me the Range Rover. A small precaution so the vehicles don't become too familiar to whomever might be watching us."

I gave him the fob for the Range Rover and took the keys to the Jag. I knew he was worried. He wanted me to have a quick getaway car, and he was also worried I might become careless and let myself be seen. I could have told him that wasn't going to happen. He had been closer to the truth earlier when he'd said I was becoming a more efficient killing machine, not less. The only danger was to my soul, not my body.

I headed toward Marina del Rey, cruising at a steady twenty-five miles per hour, and called Rosario. She answered on the first ring.

"Harry?"

I frowned. "How did you know it was me?"

"Don't be so suspicious." She laughed. "Only you have this number. Are you okay?"

"More or less. How are you?"

She gave a small laugh. "Imagine. I am devastated, but I have my father, and I am starting a new life..." She let the words trail. "Can I ask you are you alone? Where are you?"

"Let me ask you instead."

She sighed. "Don't you get tired of living like this?"

"Yes. Where are you?"

"You are alone?"

"Yes."

"Right now I am in Santa Monica. My name is Maria del Prado. I have a whole life and a past which I have to learn. I have a nice apartment with my father in a quiet, pretty street. But they tell me we will move soon. You want to come and visit with us?"

I smiled, not sure what I was feeling. "I'm on my way now."

Her voice rose in pitch. "Seriously? You are coming? How long will you be?"

Her enthusiasm made me laugh. "Half an hour tops. Give me your address."

She was in one of the new apartments on the corner of Colorado and Lincoln. She was on the fourth floor with nobody above her. I rode the elevator up, and she was standing in the doorway waiting for me. She looked relaxed and almost happy, in jeans and a simple white blouse. She came toward me and held me, and I held her back. It felt good. It felt like something I could do for a long time.

When we eventually let go, I asked her, "How's your dad?"

She gave a small shrug. "He's okay. It will take time. Buddy has found a doctor for him."

"Buddy?"

She smiled. "Your brigadier. I take him for walks, sometimes we go to the beach. Right now he is sleeping. You going to come in or we talk out here on the landing?"

She led me inside to a bright, sunny living room with lots of glass and a terrace. I sat on the sofa, and she went to the open plan kitchen.

"You want a drink?"

"No, thanks. I just had lunch with the - with Buddy."

She put an herbal teabag in a mug with a picture of a smiling sun on it, then added boiling water from a kettle. As she poured, she said, "I had a long talk with him."

"He told me."

"Did he tell you what we talked about?"

"No. He told me a lot about what he thinks. But not what you talked about."

"I am worried about you, Harry."

"It seems to be a growing club. I'm okay."

She came and sat next to me on the sofa, shaking her head. "I don't think you're okay. You don't look okay to me. I look in your eyes, and you know what I see?"

"I'm not very good at that kind of thing, Rosario -"

She seemed not to hear me. I guess the question was rhetorical because she went on, "I see exhaustion. I see a tired soul. I see a man who has fought and fought and fought, with no rest, and now he is tired in his soul, and he needs support."

I tried to answer, to tell her she was right, but the words were trapped in my chest and wouldn't budge. I shrugged instead and gave my head a twitch. She stood and went back into her kitchen. There she poured a glass of Irish and brought it to me.

"Maybe you don't want it," she said with a smile, "but I think you need it, Harry. I really wanted to talk to you before they send us to wherever they are going to send us. You know I have been thinking so much about you." She searched my eyes with a small frown. "Have you thought about me?"

"Yes."

"You do so much, Harry, to help people. You take such risks, you face danger, you never stop. Always going, thinking, acting..." She trailed off, watching my face with real sadness. "And killing. You are a soldier, fighting for justice, fighting to help the weak, life's victims. But you cannot go on like this forever. Eventually you will collapse. You need..."

Again her words died away. I said, "What?"

She shook her head. "Harry, it's like the Eagles song, you know it?" She smiled. "You gotta let somebody love you, before it's too late."

I smiled. It wasn't a happy expression because I had a huge hollow inside me. "Rosario, people who love me get hurt. I am bad news. I attract trouble."

"Until now. But you can resign, you can die, you can disappear, like me, and I can be there for you, to look after you, to care for you. It is all I have ever wanted, a strong man like you, so that I can be a good woman for him. We can do good things, we can have plans and projects, we are still young."

I laughed. "Are you proposing to me?"

Her face said she felt wounded. "Am I that ridiculous? I thought in Poman we had felt something for each other."

"I am not laughing at you, Rosario. And you are not ridiculous at all. This is just very unexpected. I have work I need to finish."

"More killing? If you are not careful, Harry, you will end up killing your soul. When will it stop?" She picked up my glass and handed it to me with a cute smile. "Drink, maybe you can relax. Will you stay with me tonight?"

I took a pull on the whiskey, savored it, and swallowed. I said, "I'm a little overwhelmed."

She placed her cup on the coffee table in front of us and covered my face gently in kisses, then she sat at my feet and started unlacing my boots.

"Overwhelmed." She said it with a small laugh, like the word was ridiculous. "But this is what life, normal day-to-day life, should be like. Affection, a few people around you, your family, who care about you." She pulled off my left boot and tossed it to one side, then set to work on my right boot. "Instead of a life of violence, a life of love and affection." She grinned at me. "You and me, looking out for each other, caring for each *other*." She stressed the last word and laughed as she tugged off my other boot, then started pulling off my socks. When she was done, she rested her arms and her chin on my knees. "Does that not sound over-whelming, my love, or does it sound good?"

I stared at her. She really was beautiful. I took another pull on the whiskey and asked myself how it would be to wake up in the morning and see her head on the pillow next to me. I thought it would be good.

I sighed and rubbed my eyes and took another sip of whiskey.

"It sounds amazing, Rosario. Unreal. But it has been so many years, such a radical change."

She nodded with her chin still resting on her forearms on my knees. "Yes, my love, you have to die. We both have to die and be reborn as new people. But not just for the outside world. We have to do it inside, in our souls too. Die and re-become as new people. People who live for love, for each other, in peace. Do you want this with me, Harry? I want it so much with you."

I took a deep breath and sighed. The more I thought about it, the harder it was to find the downside. She was warm, she was loving, she had proved herself in Poman, and man she was beautiful!

And I was so tired. I was tired of killing, tired of fighting, tired of war, tired of hardening my heart to the suffering in my victims' eyes.

"My poor baby is so tired," she said and rose to sit beside me. She put her arms around me and pulled me gently down so that my head was lying in her lap. "You stay with me now, my love. I am all yours, and you are all mine."

I was drifting, I felt at peace. It was a peace I had never experienced before in my life. Her lap was a soft pillow. Her hands were soft and stroked my face and my hair. Her voice had become a gentle murmur, like the lapping of water against a peaceful shore. Quiet voices inside my own head told me it was time to rest, time to stop fighting. The brigadier had good men working for him, the best. They would get Angela. I had contributed a good plan, now they would execute it like good, efficient professionals. I had contributed what I had. Now I was retiring.

I was retiring to a cool, quiet, dark place, deep down inside. Deep down inside I smiled and almost laughed because I knew I was going down the rabbit hole. I could see the rabbit hole. It was round and black, like a bullet hole in the side of the hill. It was more like a mountain. The mountains where I was supposed to be, in Altadena.

Going down the rabbit hole, I slipped into the dark.

TWENTY

I KNEW I WAS IN TROUBLE WHEN I OPENED MY EYES.
And I was mad at myself for my stupidity, for my absentminded-
ness and for allowing myself to slip into such a state of self-pity
that I would forget such an essential piece of information.
Colorado and Lincoln in Santa Monica were twenty-five miles as
the crow flies from the mountains in Altadena.

I was on a sofa. It was not the same sofa I had been on. This
one was suede and smelled expensive. As the awareness of my
stupidity settled, I began to become aware of other things: the
aching pain in my entire body, a feeling of nausea in my belly, and
a crippling weakness in my muscles.

I saw also a large coffee table of the sort rich people who feel
guilty about poor people buy so they can say they support ethnic
communities and fair trade. It had a coffee pot on it and two cups.
I wondered if the coffee was fair trade and realized I was still
suffering the effects of whatever drug she had fed me in my
whiskey.

A voice in my head told me, "You will die today."

I didn't rebel against that voice. I knew it was probably true.

A voice that was outside my head said, "You don't look nearly
so dangerous now, Mr. Bauer. Tell me, do you feel dangerous?"

I frowned and forced myself to focus beyond the ethnic table. I wasn't surprised to see Angela sitting curled up in a huge armchair with a glass of what looked like champagne in her hand and her small feet tucked under her.

I tried to move, but my body seemed to be made of wet sand. I didn't feel dangerous. I felt like I might suffocate quietly under my own weight. She laughed. It was a light, delighted laugh. It should have been a delightful sound, but it was sick and ugly because the delight was provoked by pain.

"It will pass," she said, "if you live long enough."

A deep, unconscious obstinacy forced me to struggle into a sitting position. My head ached and swam, and I fought down the need to vomit. She laughed again. "Oh, remarkable," she said. "I wonder if there is anything I could *not* provoke you into doing?"

My voice came out like I'd spent the last twenty years smoking sixty French cigarettes a day. I said, "Yeah, you couldn't provoke me into letting you live."

"Valiant," she said and sipped her wine. "A little pathetic, but valiant. I wonder how much this is going to hurt." She looked over to her right.

I frowned and struggled to focus. I took in a wall behind her made up of sliding plate glass doors. To her right, I could see a large, oval dining table that seemed to be made of obsidian and had a silver candlestick in the middle. Beyond that, I saw a large, white grand piano, and leaning against it, with a glass of champagne in her hand, was Rosario. She wasn't smiling. She was frowning.

She moved off the piano and approached down two shallow steps from what I now saw was a mezzanine floor. She stood behind Angela and laid one hand on her shoulder.

"You have a choice, Harry. You can die slowly, over hours, possibly days, in a great deal of pain, or you can die quickly and painlessly, in a second or two. Which do you choose?"

I closed my eyes to focus on my breathing. I took three deep breaths before opening them again.

"I choose to kill you both and make the world a better place."

Angela looked up at Rosario and placed her own hand over Rosario's on her shoulder. "He's magnificent, darling."

Now Rosario smiled. "Who do you work for, Harry? Who sent you against us?"

"Fuck you."

"We are tracking the parent corporations of the companies bidding on the mine. It is just a question of time before we get them. You may as well tell us and spare yourself a lot of pain."

I looked at her under my brows and felt the first warm stab of adrenaline in my belly. I tried to move my arms, but they were too heavy.

"Special Activities, the Central Intelligence Agency."

Rosario said, "I happen to know that's not true." She drained her glass, tipping it up high and throwing her head back. Then she leaned forward and tapped the glass on the ethnic table so that it broke into jagged pieces.

"This is going to hurt a lot, Harry. I am going to enjoy watching you weep and beg. I know how tired and emotionally damaged you are. You'll be too weak to stop me, and within thirty seconds you'll be crying like a girl, begging for death."

She came over and knelt in front of me. She set the glass on the floor and pushed up my left trouser leg. I needed to kick, to punch. I needed to react, but whatever she had given me had my muscles turned to heavy, sleeping sludge.

She smiled into my eyes. "We want to avoid any arteries or major veins. We want it to hurt a lot, but we don't want you to bleed out, do we? We want this pain to last a long time, right, Harry, my darling?"

She did it fast, and all the while, I saw her eyes fastened on mine. The pain was indescribable. She dragged the edge of the jagged glass down my shin bone, biting deep from the knee all the way down to my ankle. I don't know if it was the drug or if it was some deep, unconscious obstinacy that shaped me from the inside, but I bit down on the pain, felt my neck swell and my face burn. I held her eyes every unending second of the cut, but I made not a sound.

The adrenaline was making a fire in my belly. When she withdraw the bloodstained glass, I could see both fascination and the first smoldering of fear in her eyes. They were big, beautiful dark eyes, like the eyes of that child in Al-Landy. I curled my lip and snarled, "You can't hurt me. You don't know what pain is."

Rage welled out from my belly, and maybe that hot adrenaline in my blood counteracted the drug. Maybe I'll never know, but my snarl turned to a roar, and I got to my feet. For a moment I stood, unsteady, staring down at them, at their astonished faces.

Then everything happened at once. A massive explosion shook the house. As though in slow motion I saw, through the plate glass windows, how the trees swayed and bowed, garden chairs, tables, and parasols were hurled across the yard and smashed into the fence. I saw the glass in the sliding doors tremble and shatter. I saw Angela cowering in her chair with her arms covering her head.

Just inches in front of me, Rosario was staggering, staring at the shattered windows and the yard filling with rolling dust and smoke. I backhanded her across the head, and she fell to the floor. I bent unsteadily and grabbed the broken champagne glass. I was disoriented, but somewhere, I could hear clattering feet approaching, and I dropped to my knees in front of Angela's chair.

Two guys burst into the room shouting, "Lady Angela! Lady Rosario! We must go! We must go now!"

A second later, there were two men taking an arm each and lifting Angela out of the chair. I didn't hesitate. With an insane rage surging inside me, I got to one knee and thrust the glass deep into the neck of one of them. He screamed, and blood sprayed like a fountain across the room as he wrenched the glass from his neck and tried to stem the flow. But I was gripping his arm, pulling it away and reaching under his arm. In one single movement, drilled into me over eight years, I pulled the gun free and put four slugs in the other guy's chest.

In the chaos and confusion, I could hear a car revving. Then tires screeched, and there was automatic fire, and more explosions. I ignored it all because Angela was staring up at me from her chair. I walked unsteadily behind her. She was whimpering and sobbing. "What are you doing? What are you going to do?"

I didn't answer. I took a fistful of her hair in my left hand and dragged her over the back of the chair. As she came, I put my right arm around her neck, so her throat was in the crook of my right elbow. I gripped my left bicep with my right hand and put my left forearm around the back of her neck. It took a second to do, but as I squeezed, it took a full thirty seconds for her to go limp. Then I let her fall on her face and I stamped the blade of my right foot into the base of her skull.

Somewhere, I could hear men shouting, "Clear! Clear!"

I ignored them. Rosario was on her knees looking at me, shaking her head, weeping.

"Harry, you love me. You know you love me. I was wrong, I made a mistake. You cannot kill me. Let me -"

I don't know what she was going to ask me, because I had picked up the Glock again and put a round through the center of her forehead. As I walked away, she was still kneeling, looking astonished.

There was smoke and dust creeping everywhere, though the explosions and the shots had ceased. I walked toward the front door, knowing and not caring that I might get shot. Through the mist, a figure approached me. He was carrying a gun, but he slipped it under his arm and approached me. I frowned as I recognized the brigadier, and he put his arms around me and held me. I tried to move, but he wouldn't let me. Then there were men lowering me onto a gurney. I wanted to tell them I was okay, but I couldn't speak, and a moment later, I was enveloped by darkness.

EPILOGUE

DAYS HAD PASSED, AND WE WERE SITTING ON THE SAND with Palisades Park at the back of us. A strong breeze was coming in off the ocean. Sometimes it snatched our words and hurled them away, toward the city, other times it took the colonel's hair and spread it across her face, so she had to finger it away.

I looked at the brigadier. His gaze didn't waver. I said, "You used me. You knew Rosario was involved."

He licked his lips, then gave his head a small shake.

"Harry, the situation had spiraled out of hand. I didn't know for a fact that she was working with Angela, but I suspected it. She claimed to be desperately in love with you, yet when she thought she was not being watched, her behavior was not consistent with that claim. Not that she was having affairs or anything of that sort, but she was out a great deal, often neglecting her father, shopping and having lunch. It struck us both as inconsistent with a traumatized, lovelorn woman. So we had her followed, and she proved very hard to follow. And we began to suspect that she had a place in Los Angeles, besides the one we had given her, where she met with somebody."

"Why didn't you tell me?"

It was the colonel who answered. "Partly because we thought

you were not in a position to be objective. You had invested a lot in this woman, and she was extremely credible. But also because we believed she would detect it if you knew."

The brigadier sighed. "I want to apologize, Harry. I did not want to do what I did. And I honestly thought there was a fifty percent chance that she was genuine and had her own peculiar way of letting off steam. But the bottom line was that these people were extremely dangerous, and if they bounced back, with the intelligence they had gleaned from the Poman incident and the connections they had in DC, they could uncover us and nail us. And I do mean assassinate you, Jane, and me. They had to be stopped immediately."

"So you bugged the Jag and tracked it to her place in Santa Monica."

"And then we followed her to Angela's mansion in Beverly Hills. We moved in as quickly as we could, following your own plan, and found as always that you had done most of the job for us."

I was quiet for a while, picking up handfuls of sand and letting it slide between my fingers.

"Why did you encourage me to believe that she would be good for me?"

He heaved another big sigh. "Honestly, Harry, because I believed that if she was for real, she would have been great for you, and there was a fifty percent chance she was for real. On the other hand, Harry, even if she wasn't for real, there are millions of women in the world who are. And everything I said to you stands, whether it is with Rosario or another woman." He smiled ruefully. "One that you preferably don't meet while dismantling a slavery racket in a lithium mine."

"So I'm getting the sack?"

Colonel Jane Harrison smiled at me, and there was some warmth in her eyes.

"You resigned some time back, Harry, and we didn't let you

go. We were wrong to do that. You need to heal. You need some time to mend."

The brigadier placed a hand on my shoulder. "We will always be here for you, Harry, as your friends, come what may."

I nodded. "Thanks. The same applies."

"Any thoughts what you'll do?"

"I don't know. Maybe I'll go to the Himalayas and find me a guru." I shook my head. "I don't know. This is a big step into the void." I looked into the brigadier's eyes. "Who am I?" I said. "Who am I when I am not killing?"

Don't miss ROGUE KILL. The riveting sequel in the Harry Bauer Thriller series.

Scan the QR code below to purchase ROGUE KILL.

Or go to: righthouse.com/rogue-kill

NOTE: flip to the very end to read an exclusive sneak peak...

DON'T MISS ANYTHING!

If you want to stay up to date on all new releases in this series, with this author, or with any of our new deals, you can do so by joining our newsletters below.

In addition, you will immediately gain access to our entire *Right House VIP Library*, which includes many riveting Mystery and Thriller novels for your enjoyment!

righthouse.com/email

(Easy to unsubscribe. No spam. Ever.)

ALSO BY BLAKE BANNER

Up to date books can be found at:
www.righthouse.com/blake-banner

ROGUE THRILLERS
Gates of Hell (Book 1)
Hell's Fury (Book 2)

ALEX MASON THRILLERS
Odin (Book 1)
Ice Cold Spy (Book 2)
Mason's Law (Book 3)
Assets and Liabilities (Book 4)
Russian Roulette (Book 5)
Executive Order (Book 6)
Dead Man Talking (Book 7)
All The King's Men (Book 8)
Flashpoint (Book 9)
Brotherhood of the Goat (Book 10)
Dead Hot (Book 11)
Blood on Megiddo (Book 12)
Son of Hell (Book 13)

HARRY BAUER THRILLER SERIES
Dead of Night (Book 1)
Dying Breath (Book 2)
The Einstaat Brief (Book 3)
Quantum Kill (Book 4)
Immortal Hate (Book 5)
The Silent Blade (Book 6)
LA: Wild Justice (Book 7)

Breath of Hell (Book 8)
Invisible Evil (Book 9)
The Shadow of Ukupacha (Book 10)
Sweet Razor Cut (Book 11)
Blood of the Innocent (Book 12)
Blood on Balthazar (Book 13)
Simple Kill (Book 14)
Riding The Devil (Book 15)
The Unavenged (Book 16)
The Devil's Vengeance (Book 17)
Bloody Retribution (Book 18)
Rogue Kill (Book 19)
Blood for Blood (Book 20)

DEAD COLD MYSTERY SERIES
An Ace and a Pair (Book 1)
Two Bare Arms (Book 2)
Garden of the Damned (Book 3)
Let Us Prey (Book 4)
The Sins of the Father (Book 5)
Strange and Sinister Path (Book 6)
The Heart to Kill (Book 7)
Unnatural Murder (Book 8)
Fire from Heaven (Book 9)
To Kill Upon A Kiss (Book 10)
Murder Most Scottish (Book 11)
The Butcher of Whitechapel (Book 12)
Little Dead Riding Hood (Book 13)
Trick or Treat (Book 14)
Blood Into Wine (Book 15)
Jack In The Box (Book 16)
The Fall Moon (Book 17)
Blood In Babylon (Book 18)
Death In Dexter (Book 19)
Mustang Sally (Book 20)

A Christmas Killing (Book 21)
Mommy's Little Killer (Book 22)
Bleed Out (Book 23)
Dead and Buried (Book 24)
In Hot Blood (Book 25)
Fallen Angels (Book 26)
Knife Edge (Book 27)
Along Came A Spider (Book 28)
Cold Blood (Book 29)
Curtain Call (Book 30)

THE OMEGA SERIES
Dawn of the Hunter (Book 1)
Double Edged Blade (Book 2)
The Storm (Book 3)
The Hand of War (Book 4)
A Harvest of Blood (Book 5)
To Rule in Hell (Book 6)
Kill: One (Book 7)
Powder Burn (Book 8)
Kill: Two (Book 9)
Unleashed (Book 10)
The Omicron Kill (Book 11)
9mm Justice (Book 12)
Kill: Four (Book 13)
Death In Freedom (Book 14)
Endgame (Book 15)

ABOUT US

Right House is an independent publisher created by authors for readers. We specialize in Action, Thriller, Mystery, and Crime novels.

If you enjoyed this novel, then there is a good chance you will like what else we have to offer! Please stay up to date by using any of the links below.

Join our mailing lists to stay up to date --> righthouse.com/email
Visit our website --> righthouse.com
Contact us --> contact@righthouse.com

facebook.com/righthousebooks
x.com/righthousebooks
instagram.com/righthousebooks

EXCLUSIVE SNEAK PEAK OF...

ROGUE KILL

CHAPTER 1

MY CELL RANG. I SAT UP AND LOOKED AT THE PHONE. IT was Colonel Jane Harris, my ex head of operations. It was three in the morning. The glass in my windows was black. I put the phone to my ear.

"Jane. Is there a problem?"

"Yes." Her voice was quiet, like she didn't want to be heard. I wondered for a moment if she was drunk, but that wasn't her style.

"Where are you?"

"I need you to listen carefully and not interrupt."

"Shoot."

"I am staking out some men—"

"You're doing *what?*"

"I need your help, Harry. I haven't got time for bullshit. I am a CIA officer, remember? I think I may have been compromised, and I have nobody else to call on—"

I suppressed a rush of rage. I got as far as, "You have no one to —" and stopped. "Where are you?"

"You know the Bayonne area of New Jersey? Bergen Point? Constable Hook—"

"I know the area. Where?"

"Avenue F and East 24th Street. I'm in a dark Volkswagen Golf, right on the corner."

I had her on the bedside table and spoke as I pulled on my clothes.

"How many of them are there?"

"So far four. I don't know if they've called for backup."

"What makes you think you're compromised?"

"They're parked outside a mosque down the road. They were out of their vehicles talking, and after a while they started looking up the road. I was pretty sure they were looking at me. Then one of them made a call."

"Get out of there."

"I can't."

I shoved my Fairbairn and Sykes in my boot and pulled on my Sig Sauer P226 as I rasped, "Why the hell not? You could have eight guys there in the next two minutes. You'll be lucky if they just shoot you!" I was running down the stairs taking them three at a time. "It's going to take me half an hour minimum to get there!"

"I haven't got time to argue with you, Harry!"

"Why? What else are you doing? Watching four guys? You can't watch and talk at the same time? I need to know the facts, Jane!"

I was out the door and taking the stoop in two strides. My car was a damned TVR. Cerbera Speed Eight. It was going to stand out like a luminous dildo at a vicar's tea party. But I had no choice, and it would at least get me there fast. I slid behind the wheel and fired up the big four hundred and forty V8 engine while she told me, "These are very bad men, Harry." I floored the pedal and did zero to sixty in less than four seconds, leaving behind the stench of burned rubber. I hit Harlem River Drive closing on a hundred and didn't fishtail when I turned north.

The colonel was saying, "We have Russian Mafia here talking to Iranians, and we have identified at least four chemists among their contacts tonight. I need to know what's going down."

I snapped, "If you've been compromised, whatever they *had* going down won't go down until you are dead, or worse, abducted for interrogation."

I was doing one-twenty hurtling north beside the black river, making for the George Washington Bridge, feeling the few seconds we had trickling away.

"I know that. That's why I haven't called Buddy. He'll order me to abort. But I know, Harry, I *know* what's going down tonight is important. I *can't* walk away. It's why I called you."

"You *need* to call the brigadier!"

"*I can't!*" she hissed. "If they move in, they'll blow it!"

I thought about calling the brigadier myself. Though I had no priority access anymore, I still had his private number. But I wanted to stay connected with the colonel in case anything went down. I needed to hear everything that happened. Right on cue, she whispered, "*I have to go.*"

I hollered, "*No! Leave the call open!*" But I was shouting at a dead cell.

I crossed the George Washington Bridge like I was jet-propelled, yelling at Siri to call the brigadier. She took her time calling, and he took his time answering. My calls were no longer considered a possible emergency. I hurtled around Overpeck Park closing on a hundred and forty miles an hour with the brigadier saying to me, "Harry, this is not a good time—"

"With all due respect, sir, shut up and listen. The colonel called me ten or fifteen minutes ago. She believes she is compromised. She did not want to inform you in case you told her to abort. I am on my way. Estimated arrival five minutes. Avenue F and East 24th Street, Bayonne. She's in a dark Volkswagen Golf on the corner. She just hung up on me saying she had to go."

His reply was "Ten-four. Over," and he was gone.

I started braking as I approached the docks, and the tires complained as I turned right onto 30th Street. After that it was a fight against myself to keep the speed and the noise down. It took only a couple of seconds for me to realize that keeping a TVR quiet was never going to happen. Its looks and the sound it makes are going to get you noticed. So I found a channel that played the kind of thudding noise guys who wear shades at night like to snort coke to and turned the volume up so high my windshield started to vibrate. Then I covered the six hundred yards to East 24th in twenty seconds and turned the corner real slow. There was no sign of a Golf anywhere. I pulled up by the grass shoulder like I was stoned or drunk and sat and had a look around. I could feel my heart pounding hard high up in my chest. I ignored it and forced myself to focus on every minute detail.

There was junk and trash all around me. Open land fenced off on my right, on my left a large, windowless building, then a couple of houses and at the end, wasteland and, hidden from view by trees and a couple of cars, a building my GPS said was a mosque.

It was from that hidden area that a man now walked out. His shadow was cast long across the road by the limpid orange light from the building. He was tall, big-shouldered, in jeans and a leather jacket. He stopped in the middle of the road and stared toward me. I knew all he could see was my headlights, and all he could hear was the thudding of my music.

He looked back the way he'd come, like he was talking. Another guy, just as tall but slimmer, joined him. He didn't take long to think it through. He started walking up the road with his big pal just behind him.

Whichever way you looked at it, there was no plus side to the situation. I made a note in the back of my mind always to have a suppressed twenty-two semi in the car. But all I had right then was a 9 mm Sig and a knife sharp enough to split atoms. I toyed with the idea of plowing into them. If I let them get close enough, I could hit them at forty miles per hour in less than two seconds. But I'd be damned if I let these sons of bitches dent a twenty-year-old TVR Cerbera Speed Eight.

When they were pulling level with the hood, I made a show of trying to climb out and stumbling to the ground, clinging to the door like I had no control over my limbs. I stayed like that, on all fours, for a couple of seconds until I heard the tall, lean guy's footsteps reaching me. Then I got on one foot and one knee and grinned a stupid, drooling grin at him. His face said he didn't know whether to kick me, shoot me, or just bundle me back into my car. His pal was closing in behind him. He said something in Persian as I got to my feet and swayed dangerously. I said, "You are a *pal*" as I laughed and lurched forward.

I reached for his shoulder with my left hand, and his instinctive reaction was to grip my arm with his right. The movement of the knife was so fast he didn't even know he'd been stabbed. It went through his esophagus, his windpipe, and his spinal nerve in a quarter of a second. His friend saw him stumble and attributed it to the drunken asshole who'd just fallen against him. By the time he'd realized he was wrong, his friend had fallen to his knees with blood gushing from this throat, and it was too late. It was too late because I had stumbled past the dying man and rammed the Fairbairn and Sykes through his right eye, making a real mess of his brain.

He went down quietly. It's hard to make a noise when your speech center is all mixed up with your autonomic digestive center and your optic nerve.

I hesitated for just a moment. The thing would have been to take the Cerbera down to the mosque and get the colonel out of there fast. But making a quiet approach with a TVR Cerbera is like trying to make a silent approach with ten Harley Davidsons. So I killed the radio and the engine and sprinted down to the corner of the building from which the two guys had emerged.

The mosque was a dilapidated two-story building. At some point in the past, somebody had painted it white. Since then, it had turned an unhealthy shade of gray turned slightly yellow by two distant street lamps. I pressed up against the wall, hunkered down into the shadows, and peered around into a yard behind a wire mesh fence with a big gate in it. The gate was open and big enough for a truck to fit through. The yard was maybe thirty or forty feet long and twenty feet across, with two garages at the far end. One of those had the roller blind up, and inside I could see a dark Golf.

There was a murmur of voices, one, maybe two low and male, one female, quiet but sounding very much like the colonel when she was mad.

I slipped through the gate and took a tangent track to the door of the open garage. There I stopped and took a moment to listen. There was a guy talking. He had a deep voice and an accent. It wasn't Russian.

"We can call police," he was saying. "I need know why you are here, alone in your car, this time of night, outside our mosque."

The colonel's voice came clear and crisp. "Please do! Call the police! This is effectively kidnapping! How dare you force me in here—"

"Shut up, woman." He said it without any real feeling. "Why you are here? You are whore waiting for client? But you don't look like whore. So what? You are spy?"

"You have asked me the same, insulting, offensive question fifty times already! And I have told you that I am an American citizen and I have a perfect right to be on any American public road I please without having to give *you* an explanation! Now will you *please* give me back the keys to my—"

"I can make you talk."

I had heard enough, and the heavy silence that followed his words told me it was time to do something. I wondered for a fraction of a second how long the brigadier was going to take to get there, then I stepped into the garage, smiling.

I had expected two guys and the colonel. What I saw surprised me, and if I had known, I would have taken a different approach. But it was too late. I was committed.

Colonel Jane Harris was sitting on a low stool with her back to a work bench. Standing in front of her, leaning his back against her Volkswagen was a big guy with a big belly and a big, black beard. In that moment he was staring at me with something between contempt and indifference.

Beyond him, leaning against the far wall, were three more guys. Two of them were holding AK 12 assault rifles. The third was holding a long screwdriver, turning it over in his fingers. I noted absently that to the left of the hood there was a closed door.

I said, "It was just some drunk guy in a foreign car who had the radio on. They're giving him a good kicking right now."

By the time I'd finished, they were all frowning. The big guy said, "Who are you?"

I gave a small laugh and said, "Right?" Simultaneously, I shot the two guys with the AK12s. The guy with the screwdriver leaped and rolled behind the car, and I smashed my foot into the side of the big guy's knee. He screamed, and I yelled at Jane, "*Get your key!*"

She was on it, and I went around her car looking for the guy with the screwdriver. I found him on all fours scrabbling at the door. He was quick. I fired, but he had the door open and rolled through. I was going after him, but I could see the colonel across the roof. Her face was twisted with rage, looking down at the floor, where she appeared to be kicking the big guy.

I snapped, "Have you got the key?"

"*Yes!*" She snarled it through her teeth with one last kick.

"*Get in!*"

She wrenched open the door and clambered in. I got behind the wheel. We slammed the doors, fired up the engine, and reversed out at speed. I spun the wheel as we went ass-first out the gate and made the tires squeal as we surged up the road toward the Cerbera.

"Get ready to jump and run for the TVR!" I yanked up the handbrake and twisted the wheel so we spun on a dime and screeched to a halt, with me on the driver's side of the Cerbera and the colonel on the passenger side. I bellowed, "*Now!*" and we shoved open the doors and ran for the TVR beast.

As we did so, I heard the rattle of automatic fire behind us.

Jane yanked open the passenger door and slipped in. As I pulled open my door, I saw the Golf shudder and the windows shatter.

I got behind the wheel, made the big V8 growl, and reversed my ass into Avenue F. I slammed in first and made zero to sixty in three and a half seconds. I jumped the lights onto 440, and then we were hurtling toward I-95 and the George Washington Bridge.

I snarled at my cell, "Siri, call the brigadier!"

It rang once, then, "We're on our way. Where are you?"

"In my Cerbera headed north on I-95 toward the George Washington Bridge."

"You have Jane?"

"The colonel is with me. There are four men dead at the mosque on East 24th, one badly beaten and one armed who shot at us as we left. They have Russian AK 12s."

"You are both uninjured?"

"Yeah—"

I looked at the colonel. Her eyes were glazed, her mouth was sagging, and her skin looked yellow. I felt the acid burn of fear in my belly, but my voice was ice-cold when I said, "Correction. The colonel is hit." I reached over and felt her wrist for a pulse. I said, "Critical. Barely a pulse. We're losing her."

His voice was equally cold when he said, "I'll meet you at Teterboro with a chopper. We're on our way."

He hung up, and I floored the pedal. The Cerbera will do a hundred and ninety-five miles per hour. I think we got close on the way to the airport.

CHAPTER 2

We stood on the tarmac and watched the chopper rise into the predawn blackness. The last thing the doctor had said to the brigadier before he climbed in beside his patient was, "Prepare yourself, Buddy. She might go tonight. She's unlikely to make it."

The brigadier had nodded, like he'd been told his groceries were going to arrive fifteen minutes late. Then he turned, and we'd walked in silence back to my car.

Once there, I asked him, "Where are you taking her?"

"We have cutting-edge facilities at Pleasantville."

"Who was she investigating?"

"You know I can't tell you that, Harry. You resigned."

"You need a ride?"

He nodded. "Yes, thank you."

I didn't ask him where he wanted to go, and he didn't tell me. We just climbed in the car, I pulled out of the airport, and we headed for Manhattan. We covered the distance in silence, crossed from Fort Lee to Fort Washington, came off onto Riverside Drive, and slowly ambled down to Broadway as far as 133rd before turning west and weaving my way home, all in absolute silence.

Finally I pulled up outside my brownstone and killed the

engine. The sky was turning pale, and the streetlamps were burning against a clear sky. I said, like I was talking to the steering wheel, "I didn't ask, but I figured you could use a drink. You want breakfast?"

Now I looked at him, and he nodded. "Yes, breakfast and a shot would be good. Thank you."

I let him in and closed the door, and he followed me into the kitchen, where he sat at the big pine table while I scrambled eggs, made coffee, and poured us each a stiff shot of Bushmills.

I finished the eggs and toast and placed his plate in front of him. He nodded, and I noticed he hadn't touched his whiskey or his coffee. I raised my glass.

"Cheers!"

His eyes searched my face for a couple of seconds before he replied.

"Yes, cheers!"

He knocked it back, set down his glass, and picked up his fork.

"Harry, you left Cobra. I can't tell you anything about what Jane was doing."

I frowned as I chewed. I swallowed, drained my cup, and refilled it.

"Sir, everything Cobra does is completely illegal. We—you— murder people routinely in breach of the laws of every democracy in the Western world, but you are concerned about breaking Cobra's own rules on confidentiality? Rules that don't even have the status of laws?"

He sighed and forced himself to eat some of the egg.

"It may seem absurd to you, Harry—"

"There is no 'may' about it, sir. Forgive me for being blunt, but it's stupid. It is the exact antithesis of what you drilled into us every day. Prepare and train as much as is humanly possible, but once you are in the field, be prepared to adapt and improvise at a moment's notice."

He stared at me a moment and said, "Adapt and improvise" with no particular intonation.

"You always told us the objective was to win, and to win, we must use every resource available to us."

"Yes," he said and stuffed egg in his mouth. "Every available resource."

"I am an available resource, sir. You know I am good, and you know you can trust me. Use me."

"You chose to resign. Why this now?"

"You know the answer to that as well as I do. This is the colonel..." I trailed off, searching for words that would both convey the pain and the fear we were both feeling but at the same time hide those very things. In the end, I said, "We owe it to her."

"Yes," he said and picked up his cup.

"We are from the Regiment, sir. We are blades. We do things differently. Our way."

"All right, Harry. We are going to have a conversation that never happened. It never happened because after breakfast I called for my car and left."

"That's what happened."

"So it would have been impossible for us to have this conversation."

"What conversation?"

He smiled in a way that spoke more of weariness than humor. "Have you heard of a man called Nick Galkin?"

I shook my head. "No, never."

He nodded in an abstracted way, looking at the kitchen floor. "He keeps a pretty low profile. His father was Russian. He claimed to have worked for the KGB, but when the Soviet Union collapsed, he moved into the private sector, where he became a modest billionaire, moved to the United States, and married an American woman of breeding. Daddy is the kind of man who makes and unmakes presidents. So young Nick was already a very powerful man before he was even born, in 1990."

"That makes him 34."

"And a billionaire in his own right."

"How does he make his money?"

"That is a good question, and one we and the CIA spent many, many man-hours on. In brief, it goes something like this: Nick has created a number of shell companies on off-shore fiscal havens. In practically all of these cases, the companies are owned by other companies which are in turn owned by corporations. So they are hard to track down."

"Okay. What does he do with these companies?"

"In essence, what he does is identify countries that have trade embargos against them. Let's say, for example, that sanctions against a Middle Eastern country mean it can't sell oil to some of its usual trading partners—say France and Germany, the European Union. But the tiny Pacific Island of King George has no such embargo against—let's call it Iraqistan. So Nick has a trading company registered in King George, and he buys from Iraqistan a couple of oil tankers' worth of crude oil."

"He still can't sell it to Europe because the provenance is Iraqistan."

"Correct, but what he can do is sell it to the White Russian Trading Corporation, which is registered on the island of Bintan in Indonesia. From there, the cargo is transferred to another ship, where the bill of lading shows the petroleum as being bought and sold in Indonesia, and from there, through perhaps another couple of buyers and sellers, all belonging to our Nick, the goods arrive after a short delay, though at a considerably higher price, in Europe."

We sat in silence for a while. Then I said, "If the product you're dealing with is oil, you can almost write it off as a resourceful man surviving in the dog-eat-dog world of international commerce." The brigadier nodded. I said, "But something tells me we are not just talking about oil."

"That something would be dead right. With the help of his father, he has spent some twenty years building up a network of shell companies and holding corporations that defy Western jurisdiction. He can pretty much move anything anywhere he wants. And he has made three very big, very powerful friends—"

"China, Russia, and Iran."

"Intelligence from all the Five Eyes and Israel suggests very strongly that he is moving not just chemicals for chemical weapons but essential components for nuclear bombs. But nobody can prove it. The CIA approached us through Jane and asked us to take care of him but also to try and get some access to his network—either to close him down or destroy it. It's not a needle in a haystack, quite the opposite. It's more like a three-dimensional spiderweb enmeshed in a haystack."

"And that's what Jane was doing?"

He looked at me for a long time. He looked gray and drawn.

"That's her job, Harry. She's a highly capable CIA officer. She would not thank me for treating her like an incompetent girl."

"I know that."

He frowned. "I don't understand quite why she called you, and it was you who called me..." He shook his head. "Why didn't she call me directly for backup?"

I gave a smile you could call rueful. "I asked her the same question while I was falling down the stairs pulling my clothes on. She said she was worried you'd abort the mission."

"She was right. And I think the outcome shows it would have been the right decision." He reached across the table and gripped my wrist. "That is no reflection on you, Harry. What you did was extraordinary in itself. Nobody could have guarded against what was ultimately a lucky shot. Or an unlucky one, depending on who you are..." He trailed off.

I nodded. "What's that old Viking thing? Fearlessness is better than a faint heart for any man who would poke his nose out of doors. The length of my life and the day of my death were fated long ago."

"By the Norn, indeed. Let us stay positive and believe firmly that that day has not come yet for Jane."

We drank to that, and I distributed more whiskey.

"So brass tacks, sir."

He gave his head a twitch. "It's not quite that easy. The way I see it, the mission comes in two parts. The first part is well within your capability."

"Kill him and his immediate ring."

"Yes, but the second part is more complicated. Close down his network."

"I can do that."

He frowned at me. "How, for God's sake?"

"I need to talk to your smartest IT nerd. We need to put together a virus that combines the worst elements of the worst viruses to date." I counted some off on my fingers. "Stuxnet, Cryptolocker, Zeus, Mydoom."

"For what purpose, precisely?"

"To identify his companies using artificial intelligence and spread through them, shutting them down as it goes. Any funds found in their accounts are diverted to Cobra, and I trust you to give me fifty percent as spoils of war."

"That's fair enough, but there is the small matter of the delivery system. How on earth do you plan to deliver this mega-virus?"

"That's the simplest part of all, sir. He will introduce it into his system himself, only he will think it is money he is receiving. But the figure will be a code for the virus to ride in piggyback and invisible."

He was quiet for a long time. Finally he said, "That is actually a very good idea. You would pose as a client, representing a major commercial interest. You buy the product and pay. The virus rides in on the money."

He stabbed at his scrambled eggs with his fork for a while, then drank his coffee and finished his Bushmills. Finally he set down his glass and sighed.

"Harry. This could work. I am going to talk to our IT department. They may want to have a discreet word with you. Meanwhile I'll have a copy of the colonel's file sent over. We are not employing you, so you shall have to decide yourself who goes down and who is allowed to live."

I shrugged and made a face. "In my experience, people tend to do that themselves."

He nodded. "Your body count was talked about at the mess in the Regiment, and now it is discussed at Cobra. No complaints from me." He stood. "I'll be in touch later today."

He called for his car, and ten minutes later, I watched him walk to the Bentley, climb in, and drive away. He had offered me a number I could call to stay up to date with the colonel's progress, but I declined. I figured as long as nobody called me, that would be good news.

I told him, "Let me know when she's out of surgery. The rest we'll take a day at a time."

I closed the door on the morning and lay on the sofa in the bay window turning things over in my mind. Getting close to Nick Galkin was not going to be easy, and I wondered if the colonel had developed any kind of plan herself. The answer came twenty minutes later when a biker rang the bell and handed me a sealed parcel.

When I opened it, it contained evidence of what I had always known: that the colonel was thorough to the point of being fastidious and highly organized.

Much of her research I had already been through with the brigadier. In addition to that, there were photographs of a large number of men, including the four I had killed that night, the one she had seriously maimed or killed herself, and the one who had ultimately shot her. These, and a number of others, were listed as Iranian intelligence staff attached to the Iranian Permanent Mission to the United Nations.

She had intelligence from the CIA that Nick Galkin was in New York and had attended several meetings both at the UN and at private apartments. His meetings made interesting reading.

He had visited Arav Yasdi, the secretary to the ambassador on several occasions, both at the UN Building and at Third Avenue.

What was more interesting was his three meetings with Xie Ken, the Chinese Ambassador to the United Nations. One of those had been at the UN, and the other two had been at the Plaza Hotel. Those meetings constituted what President Bush in his day would have called the Axis of Evil: a Russian ex-KGB officer meeting with high-ranking Iranian and Chinese diplomats in private. It was interesting but not surprising.

What was surprising was his series of meetings with Stavros Moustakas, the European Union's Ambassador to the United Nations, not to mention the private meetings at the private apartments of Adam Schmidt, the first secretary to the secretary for defense of the German Federal Republic. That was on the Monday. On the Wednesday, he'd dined with M Julia Garnier, the personal secretary to the Minister of the Armed Forces of France. And Friday, he had dined at the palatial home of Oscar Hansen on 69th Street. Hansen was the famous, infamous, and notorious Danish arms dealer, notable among other things for helping to establish the largest Buddhist temple in Europe. At that same dinner, there had been CEOs and heads of department from the McDaniels Skyline Rat Labs, Anglo-American Petrochemicals, Global Chemicals of Texas, and Nevada Delivery Systems, to name but a few.

I spoke aloud, absently, like the colonel was sitting in the chair across from me.

"So if we assume, just for a moment, that the Axis of Evil—Iran, Russia, and China—are Nick Galkin's clients, and we take a look at the other people he has been talking to, what do we find they have in common?"

The words hung in the air because there was nobody to answer them. I raised my thumb. "The French and the German were attached to their respective ministries of defense; the Dane is an arms dealer. Then, the notable guests at the major function that week and the Danish arms dealer's house were McDaniels Skyline Rat Labs, Anglo-American Petrochemicals, Global Chemicals of Texas, and Nevada Delivery Systems, all defense contractors, all at the cutting edge of military technology, and all part of what Dwight Eisenhower had termed the Military-Industrial Complex.

"So what does that mean?" I asked the air. "That American defense contractors are selling cutting-edge military technology to our enemies?"

I read on. The colonel had believed to begin with that Iran was trying to build a dirty bomb or some kind of biological or chemical weapon that it could deploy against Israel. But the more research she had done and the further she had investigated, the clearer it had become that this went well beyond a single weapon.

I paused and closed my eyes. My memory was reaching for something a Dutch Admiral in NATO had said recently. The guy had the same name as me: Bauer. And he had said that the civilian population should prepare, because war with Russia had become inevitable.

Scan the QR code below to purchase ROGUE KILL.
Or go to: righthouse.com/rogue-kill

Made in United States
Orlando, FL
02 January 2026

76166237R00116